An Echo at Ebbets Field

Revised edition

By

Jeremiah Baldonado

And

Richard Williams

Baldonado Brothers Books

The Hometown Players

(in order of appearance)

Danny Boone, second base. The world's biggest Dodger fan. Obsessed with baseball. Bats right, throws right.

Napoleon Buonaparte, starting pitcher. The Emperor of France who almost conquered the world. Talkative on the mound; nice breaking ball. Throws left.

Arthur Wesley, catcher. The Duke of Wellington. A big reason why the above listed pitcher didn't conquer the world, but instead met his Waterloo. Fair hitter, great throw to second. Bats right, throws right.

Christina Rosetti, bookshop owner and poet. Not a baseball player. Sensitive, intelligent, and a beautiful soul.

Jacob, town Mayor. In charge of town but also seems to have other universal connections.

Daniel Boone, frontiersman. Trailblazing wilderness expert and fierce in battle. Sometimes confused with others of the same name and birthdate.

Abraham Lincoln, first base. 16th President of the United States, who saved the Union by winning the Civil War. Good fielder, power hitter. Bats right, throws right.

Andrew Johnson, 17th President of the United States. Gifted and talented tailor; impeached but narrowly acquitted to continue holding office.

Frederick Douglass, third base. Man of God, intellectual, author, pioneer for civil rights. Fearless player. Outstanding fielder, strong line drive hitter. Bats right, throws right.

Martha Jane Cannary, right field. Legend of the old west; also known as Calamity Jane. Throws right, bats right, good field.

William Butler Hickok, outfield. Gunfighter and cowboy, also known as Wild Bill. Average arm; fair hit. Throws right, bats right.

Cathay Williams, shortstop. Female soldier in the Civil War and on the Frontier. Good field, strong hitter. Throws right, bats right.

Simon Bolivar, pitcher. The great liberator of South America. Strong velocity; excellent control. Throws right, bats right.

Charles Babbage, manager. Mathematician and inventor of the computer. Analytical statistics master.

John Marshall, Head umpire. Chief Justice, United States Supreme Court. Not an easy man to argue with.

Yoshida Shoin, outfield. Master teacher and samurai. Excellent speed and power. Throws right, bats right.

Alexander Dumas, Patisserie shop co-owner. Author and national treasure of France.

Victor Hugo, Patisserie shop co-owner.
Author and national treasure of France. Tends to be
competitive with his partner.

Oscar Wilde, center field. Irish author,
intellectual, poet, playwright. Great field, strong
hitter. Throws left, bats left.

Charles Dickens, shortstop. English author,
poet, philanthropist. Antique enthusiast. Strong
fielder, reliable place hitter. Throws right, bats right.

The Visitors

(in order of appearance)

Dinah, Mayor of the visitor's town. Daughter of Jacob. Shrewd negotiator, with a few universal connections of her own.

Frank Chance, first base. Played for Chicago Orphans, later called the Cubs. Two World Series championships. Skilled prizefighter, also a successful manager. Bats right, throws right.

Ty Cobb, center field. Legendary fierce competitor. Scored and batted in the most run in history. Bats left, throws right.

Smokey Joe Wood, starting pitcher. Said by many to be the fastest pitcher who ever lived. Bats right, throws right.

George Herman (Babe) Ruth, middle relief pitcher. One of the best young pitchers who ever lived. He once pitched 9 shutouts in a season. Due to a player shortage in World War I, he began to play daily and became slightly better known as hitter. Bats left, throws left.

John McGraw, Manager. A smart manager known to win at any cost; thrown out of 132 games over his career.

Heinie Groh, third base. A great fielder with a famous "bottle" bat, with which he terrorized opposing teams. Throws right, bats right.

Honus Wagner, shortstop. Considered to be the greatest shortstop of all time; won 8 straight batting titles. Throws right, bats right.

Napoleon Lajoie, second base. He was so popular that one team named itself after him. He holds the all-time American League batting average season record of .426. Bats right, throws right.

Connie Mack, catcher. Was a catcher, manager, and owner. Thought by many to be the smartest player who ever lived. Throws right, bats right.

Tris Speaker, left field. Arguably the most accomplished all around outfielder in history. His glove was known as "the place triples go to die". Throws left, bats left.

Sam Crawford, right field. Teammate and rival of Ty Cobb. Known to be almost a perfect player and decent man, he still holds the record for the most triples in one season. Throws right, bats right.

Stuffy McInnis, first base. Part of the legendary "$100,000 infield" of the Philadelphia Athletics. A feared line drive hitter. Bats right, throws right.

John Henry Lloyd, second base. Star player of the Negro Leagues; said by Babe Ruth to be the greatest player to ever play the game. Throws right, bats left.

Burleigh Grimes, closing relief pitcher. The last pitcher legally allowed to throw a spitball;

described as a truly menacing presence on the
mound.   Throws right, bats right.

Chapter 1

The springtime sun was setting over the left field wall of the baseball diamond, just behind a scoreboard showing a 4-4 tie. It was a perfect April afternoon in Arizona, in the bottom of the ninth inning with two out. The score was tied, the bases were loaded, and Danny Boone stepped up to bat. He knew he should have been nervous, but he wasn't. *Just get on base*, he thought. *How hard can that be? You don't need a home run. You don't need a double. You don't even need a single. A walk, a dropped third strike, a bunt- anything that will put me on base bring the runner on third home and wins the game.*

Danny wasn't cocky- just confident. He was 14, but had worked harder and put in more time practicing than any local 18 year old. He was ready for this. He wasn't nervous, but the relief pitcher just brought in clearly was. Being brought into the final inning of a league championship game was tough, and it showed in the pitcher's face. His glove trembled just a little as he leaned in and looked at the catcher. He shook his head, then shook it again.

Finally, the nervous boy seemed to settle on a pitch. He checked the runners and began his windup. Danny heard his name shouted from the dugout. He crowded the plate slightly. The ball was released high, and the pitch was faster and wilder than anything he had seen all season. He tried to adjust, tried to move, tried to get out of the way, but couldn't avoid the ball slamming into the left side of his batting helmet. His helmet flew off, and he began to travel and suddenly felt as if he were leaving the earth even as his body crumpled and fell limp. Lights flashed. A voice came like a distant echo. We won, it whispered quietly. The voice faded, and everything became a very silent, dark, dark blue.

Chapter 2

He kept hearing a ball hit a mitt. Again and again, there was a slight grunt of effort from whoever was throwing- and a split second later, a *thunk!* as the ball struck leather. Only, it wasn't really the exact sound of a ball hitting a mitt. It didn't actually sound like a ball at all- just something thrown and hitting something else, every few seconds.

It got louder. He opened his eyes and felt soft grass under his back. The sun was out. It felt like late morning on a clear, warm day. He sat up and touched his head. It felt fine. He looked around and saw he was in the middle of a meadow. The grass was almost flat, and it was surrounded by a forest. It reminded him of a baseball field. This is just about the size of Dodger Stadium, he thought. Almost exactly. He looked to out to his right and pictured the aluminum roof shading the right field bleachers. He remembered once catching a Cory Seager home run there, leaping up and spearing the ball with his glove. He tried to remember when it was and who was there with him, but couldn't.

He heard the *thunk!* again and turned toward the sound. He saw a young man standing in front of one of the larger trees. The man was about 5'6", and had a stout, athletic build. Next to him was a large pile of stones. He picked them up one at a time and threw them at the tree. He was a lefty, and he never missed. The stones had carved out a small ring of chipped bark and exposed wood no more than 6 inches around. Danny stood and walked toward him. The young man looked to be in his early twenties. He wore a loose-fitting, old-fashioned linen shirt with a high collar, and pants that clung to his legs, stopping at mid-calf. He wore black boots that came over his pants up to the knee. Danny had never seen anyone with such clothing, and then glanced down at himself. He noticed that he wore roughly the same outfit, except that his shirt was a medium blue. It was comfortable, but he was not used to the boots and walked stiffly.

The stone thrower bent to pick up another rock, then stopped and turned to face Danny as he approached.

"*Bonjour*", he said. "I haven't seen you here before. No one new has been here for a very long time."

Though Danny could somehow tell that the man was speaking French, he was able to understand him perfectly.

"Where am I?" He asked his new acquaintance.

"In the forest meadow near our village, where we have always been."

"Where is that?"

The man laughed. "I am not sure. As time passes, it seems I know less and less and, quite frankly, care less and less. Sometimes I even forget where I was from before I came here."

"What do you remember?", asked Danny.

"I am sure that I am from Corsica, an island in the Mediterranean which is part of France. So, I call myself a Corsican, but even more a Frenchman." As he spoke, his face changed from friendly to intense and even angry. For a moment there seemed to be something frightening about him. Then he laughed. "I think before I came here I was a soldier. I am not sure." He looked at Danny and said "You are very young. What name are you called?"

"I'm Danny. What is your name?"

"I am Buonaparte. I think my Christian name is Napoleon."

Danny felt something stir in his memory, and wrinkled his brow trying to complete the thought. It seemed so hard to remember anything. "I've heard of you. You lived a long time ago and were a great French general. I can't seem to remember very well."

The young Corsican laughed again. "I doubt it. I often have dreams of fighting in the army, but I remember only being a Corsican lieutenant, and not a great one at that. I don't think I took orders very well."

He pointed to a small cobblestone road heading into the forest and smiled. "Follow me, and we will take our little army down the lane and conquer the village." With that, he picked up one last rock and threw hard and fast, hitting the bare patch on the tree dead center.

They started to walk, but before they left the meadow Danny stopped. He pointed at the cleanly chipped target on the tree.

"Where did you learn to throw like that?"

The young lieutenant shrugged. "I skipped rocks on the beach for hours at a time as a boy. I enjoy it. I always have."

"You've got a great arm", said Danny as they were walking.

Napoleon stopped and held out his left arm. "It looks like an ordinary arm," he replied. He looked puzzled, not understanding Danny's simple figure of speech.

They walked for a moment, and Danny spoke with concern. "It bothers me that I can't remember much. I can't seem to remember where I am from, either."

A cool breeze whispered through the trees as they walked through the green forest. Danny had never walked on cobblestones, and the round, uneven stones took some getting used to. Up ahead, the road led out of the forest and into the sunshine again. A small village of wooden houses appeared in the distance.

A horse-drawn cart driven by a tall, slender young man pulled onto the road ahead from a nearby field. He seemed to steer away from them, but then broke into a smile and slowed down to talk. A closer look showed the field was actually a thriving farm with fruit trees and rows of vegetables as far as the eye could see. The cart was overflowing with freshly picked produce. The driver waved.

"Top of the morning, Napoleon", said the driver, speaking with smooth Irish brogue. He wore the same type of white linen shirt as the two of them, loose fitting and comfortable.

"Hello, Arthur," replied Napoleon. He gestured to Danny. "This is Danny. He's new".

The driver raised an eyebrow in surprise. "New? It's been years since anyone new has come." He extended his hand. "Arthur Wesley, born in Dublin."

They shook hands. Napoleon spoke to Arthur. "He's got the memory fog, like all of us. But maybe that's for the better."

Arthur reached down and patted Danny's arm reassuringly. "Don't let it scare you. We all get it. The less you remember, the easier things are. When I first came here, I don't know why but I couldn't even say hello to Napoleon without getting angry. Just now, I had a feeling to turn away from the two of you. I still have no idea of what bothered me, and I don't understand why I kept referring to myself back then as Wellington instead of Arthur. Things are much better now- I even like to see him! Now climb up here. The village is still a long way away."

They hoisted themselves onto the only area of the flat wood not covered with fruits and vegetables. They swayed back and forth while listening to the *clip clop* of the horse walking steadily toward the village.

Chapter 3

The ride was longer than Danny expected. By the time they reached town, the sun was directly overhead. Wellington stopped the wagon in the middle of an ornate town square. A large, white, columned fountain topped by a statue of a weeping angel bubbled quietly in the center of the square.

Danny jumped from the wagon and looked around. People strolled through the square, smiling and speaking quietly to each other. There were men and women, all seeming to be in their late twenties or early thirties. It was quite odd. Nobody was old, and nobody was young. He walked by a store window, saw his reflection, and did a doubletake. He didn't look 14 anymore. He was now a grown man. He seemed about the same age and Napoleon and Arthur. Napoleon looked at him and smiled.

"I bet you look different than you expected."

Danny couldn't find his voice. He nodded uncertainly.

The Frenchman smiled. "All of us look different. And we don't get older or younger. It takes getting used to."

"I still don't know where I am," said Danny. "But for some reason, it doesn't bother me. I feel…"

Napoleon interrupted and finished the sentence for him. "Calm. At peace. We all do. What is the last thing you remember?"

Danny strained to remember. A faint memory, almost like an echo, came to him. "I was in a baseball game. I don't know what happened. Am I dead?"

Napoleon laughed. "You don't look like the dead men I've seen. You move too much! Plus, there are no wounds. I am not certain of where we are, but I don't feel dead."

He patted Danny's shoulder, and smiled again. "Come on. Let me introduce you to some friends. Everyone will be happy to see a new face for a change."

They walked around the square. There were many people, but it did not seem crowded. After a few quick introductions, Napoleon stopped to chat with a young woman. Danny took the opportunity to slip away down a nearby cobblestone street to collect his thoughts. The town looked as if it were from an old history book, but seemed almost too clean and perfect to be real. There were no big stores—just small brick and wood shops, with hand-lettered signs. Each shop had a small window display: one with clothing on dummies; another with bread and pastries; another had fruits and vegetables. The signs were small and crude, and often misspelled.

As he walked, he noticed a small bookshop. A thought itched at the corner of his mind, then he perked up. *I like reading!* He was as excited by the memory as he was about going somewhere that felt familiar. Inside, a small woman with both elbows on the counter stood behind a display of books. Her long hair was brown, and her skin a pale white against a simple dark blue dress. Her eyes were pleasant and friendly, but she was not smiling. She was leaning over the counter, writing with a small feather which she intermittently dipped in ink. As he approached, he glanced at the paper. She appeared to be writing verses of a poem and was concentrating fiercely on her composition.

"Hello," said Danny.

She jumped and looked up. "Good afternoon," she said after recovering from her surprise. "May I help you?"

"I was walking past and saw your shop." Books filled the nicely arranged shelves, with familiar names printed on the binding. The inside of the shop smelled clean and fresh. He looked at the binding of the books and read: Shakespeare, Dickens, Emerson, Poe, Wilde and many others. "I'm Danny. I don't know the town very well. I like to read, so I wanted to come in. This is a beautiful bookstore."

The complement seemed to unsettle her a little. "Thank you. Hardly anyone comes in here. I usually just write to pass the time. I'm Christina. "

"I saw you writing. Are you an author?"

"Yes. I write poems. Not as well as I would like, though."

He pointed to the paper. "Is that a new poem?" He asked.

She shook her head. "It's one I wrote many years ago, and sometimes I have trouble remembering it. It's in a book of mine, but I keep thinking I should be able to remember it by heart. So, I try to write it as frequently as I can. It helps me understand where we are."

"Can I read it?" He asked. If it helped Christina, maybe it would help him, too.

She turned the paper toward him. Her handwriting was beautiful and easy to read. He read the poem name out loud. "Uphill".

She smiled again. "We used to say it more slowly, which is why it looks different on paper." He noticed the word was hyphenated. "Up-Hill", he read again more slowly.

"You have a nice voice for reading", she told Danny. "Keep going. It's supposed to be a conversation. I'll read every other line."

Danny started with the first line of the first verse, and she read her lines with a soft, thoughtful voice.

Does the road wind up-hill all the way?

Yes, to the very end.

Will the day's journey take the whole long day?

From morn to night, my friend.

But is there for the night, a resting place?

A roof for when the slow dark hours begin.

May not the darkness hide it from my face?

You cannot miss that inn.

Shall I meet other wayfarers at night?

Those have gone before.

Then must I knock, or call when just in sight?

They will not keep you waiting at that door.

Shall I find comfort, travel sore and weak?

Of labour you shall find the sum.

Will there be beds for me and all who seek?

Yes, beds for all who come.

Danny finished reading and looked up at Christina. She was looking down quietly, and her eyes were wet with tears. "What's wrong?" He asked. She looked at him and then past him, through the small window into the street.

"I think that's where we are. In our resting place. I can't be sure, but I don't know how long I've been here or exactly when I came. We all keep busy, and we're all happy, but I am fighting not to forget that there was more. More sorrow, but more happiness. More pain, but more exhilaration. More defeats, but also more victories. I miss those highs and lows."

For the first time since he awoke in the field, Danny began to feel uneasy. His heart began to pound, and his insides began to knot. It seemed like panic was taking root in his mind and pushing everything else out. He was about to reply, and then heard a voice from the doorway behind him.

"Daniel. It's so good to finally meet you." It was a mature man's voice. He turned and saw an older man. He was at least 20 years senior to anyone he had yet encountered in the town. The man then looked past Danny and spoke to the woman in a calm, soothing voice.

"Christina", he said softly. "Are you upset again?" She said nothing, but looked away, the tears now streaming down her cheeks. "You must not do this to yourself. There is nothing here to provoke such sadness."

She shook her head and turned away. The stranger placed a powerful but gentle hand on Danny's shoulder. Immediately the boy felt his heart slow back to normal and his insides relax. "May I speak to you in my office next door? I am Jacob, the Mayor of our village, and I'd like to spend a little time with you." He turned to the woman, with her back still to him. "I'll be back later to check on you, Christina. Please do try to enjoy your shop and these wonderful books. I'll have more delivered today."

When the Mayor said this, Danny thought he saw Christina flinch, but she said nothing. He followed the Mayor from her shop and into the nicely windowed and sunlit office next door. It was sparsely furnished. There was an old wooden desk, a wooden file cabinet, and a small oak chair opposite the desk. There was a single piece of paper on the desk.

"Please sit." He walked behind the desk and picked up the paper, reading briefly and then looking up, looking a bit puzzled. "You're late. So to speak. I expected to meet you quite some time ago."

"I don't understand", said Danny, looking baffled. "I'm only 14. How late could I be?"

The Mayor started to speak, and then stopped, looking puzzled. His brow creased. He looked again at the paper. "Your birthdate is November 2? "

"That's me. I was born November 2, 2005."

The man looked surprised. "No. You must be forgetting. It was November 2, 1734. You are Daniel Boone. And you should have joined us in 1820 after a particularly poorly cooked meal of sweet potatoes."

Danny started to feel dizzy and hot. *Daniel Boone? Joined us?* His feet tingled. He struggled to think, but everything in his mind was foggy. "I would never eat a sweet potato. My grandpa says they make him throw up. I don't know anything about 1734. I was at bat in the league championship game, and the bases were loaded." He felt light and weak, and it was hard to get the words out, or even sit upright in the chair. He tried to speak again. "He threw a wild pitch, and it hit…" Before he could finish, he tumbled to the floor, falling into a well of spinning water and far away voices. And suddenly again, it was quiet and everything was again a deep, dark blue.

Chapter 4

Somewhere very, very far from the town Danny was in, icy winds blew as the sun was setting. The location of this place could not be described in terms of time or distance. A long-limbed man strode quickly up an icy mountainside. It was twilight and getting very cold. The man wore layers of clothing fashioned from animal hides, and the outermost layer was the skin of a sabretooth tiger, complete with the angry and imposing head forming the hood. He was being chased, and as quickly as he moved, he could hear the closely following band of men, grunting and screaming with effort. He heard what he recognized as a giant cave bear roar a few hundred feet above him. He carried a spear and knife made from the teeth of the tiger, as well as a tomahawk lashed together with some of the tiger skin. He stopped moving for a moment to try to place the bear above him and track the band of pursuers below. As he started to move again, he spoke grimly to himself.

"I don't know where I am, but it sure ain't Kentucky. Daniel, my boy, don't quit."

At the same time, even farther away, so far that thousands of miles could not even begin to measure, two people sat in a dim room near a bed. They said nothing, slumped in an agonizing posture of sorrow and defeat. In the bed was a 14-year-old boy with bandages wrapped around his head like a white turban. Both eyes were swollen shut with large purple circles around each, and traces of dried blood could be seen tracing a path from the left ear canal. A tube protruding from his mouth was connected to a ventilator, keeping his breathing regular. He made no response to any word or touch. A small screen above him showed a regular, steady heartbeat. The woman held his hand, and every so often she gave his hand a gentle squeeze, leaned forward and whispered into the swollen ear:

"Danny. Wake up."

Chapter 5

"Danny. Wake up." He heard the voice and opened his eyes. There were other voices, speaking in low, concerned tones.

The spinning stopped, and the echo of voices drew closer to Danny as his eyes opened. The Mayor stood over him, looking concerned. Behind him was Napoleon, standing next to Arthur.

Napoleon spoke, clearly worried. "*Mon frère*. Are you feeling better? We came looking for you and found you here on the ground." He reached down and brought Danny to a sitting position. The man sat for a moment, clearly embarrassed.

"I don't know what happened," Danny stammered.

"It's my fault, I'm afraid," said the Mayor apologetically "Too much information, too fast and with too little thought on my part."

"Why were you asking me those questions?" Danny asked. The Mayor shook his head.

"It appears,", he stated, "That we have the wrong Daniel Boone. That would explain your late arrival. Your exact name match along with the same day and month of birth has resulted in your appearance here. It was a preventable but understandable error."

Danny dreaded the answer, but he asked anyway: "Where exactly is here?"

The Mayor reluctantly replied. "I try not to focus too much on the where and when. It leads one to the kind of melancholia Christina suffers from. Let us just say we are 'here' and 'now'."

Danny pressed on. "If I'm the wrong person, then why can't I go home?"

The Mayor was sympathetic but firm. "These things always correct themselves over time, but we cannot control how or when. It may be a long time before the universe fixes its error."

Danny started to speak again, but the Mayor seemed to know what he was going to say and cut him off.

"For now, let's focus on things you like. Things that can help the time to pass and make you happy. I take it you're not exactly an outdoorsman or hunter like the Daniel I was expecting."

"No," said Danny, "But I like sports."

"Ah", said the Mayor. "You like to compete in physical activities. As do I. I once wrestled a friend on the side of a river for an entire night. Beat him, too. It felt good, but I injured my hip. What kind of sport do you like?"

"Mainly one. Baseball.", said Danny.

"Base, ball?", asked the Mayor, separating the two words.

"No", said Danny. "Baseball. One word. It's a sport. The first game was played in 1846 in New Jersey."

"Well," smiled the Mayor in a way that suggested he knew more than he was letting on. "Let me look into it, and let's play the baseball."

With that, he showed the three of them out, and closed his office door. Arthur, Napoleon, and Danny walked back to the town square and stood for a moment.

"An eventful first day, my good man", said Arthur. "You may need some rest. He pointed down one of the cottage lined side streets to a brown cabin composed mainly of logs. "That's the only empty cottage in town. We've all wondered at times whom it is for. I think it must be yours."

Danny looked down the lane. He was no longer surprised by anything about this town, and the sight of a roughhewn log cabin at the end of a street of genteel cottages did not shock him, nor did the fact that it was apparently his to live in all on his own. The afternoon had been longer than he thought, and dusk was setting in. He bid the two other men goodbye for the night and walked toward the cabin. He'd almost forgotten he was still carrying Christina's book. Without stopping he turned the book over and read the title: *Goblin Market and other poems*. He shook his head. With a title like that, no wonder she gets upset so easily.

The door was unlocked; in fact, there was no lock. He walked into the cabin and in one corner found what appeared to be a collection of new 19th century guns and wilderness tools. Muskets, two flintlock pistols, large knives in sheaths, blankets, a few broad brimmed felt hats, and cooking instruments lay in front of him on a nicely organized wooden table. It was obviously set for the other Daniel Boone. On the other side of the cabin was a long cot with a colorful blanket in one corner. There was a pair of soft, cotton pajamas laid out on the bed just like his mom used to do for him when he was little. He climbed into the pajamas, which were just his size, lay down, and was in a deep sleep before he could think any more about the day.

Danny dreamed he was back in a batting cage. The machine was rhythmically throwing the balls to him, and he seemed to be hitting every pitch. Each time the ball shot out of the machine, he took the perfect swing and hit the ball square. The contact made a deeper, more wooden sound than he was used to hearing, but he couldn't seem to miss. This continued for a while, and when he finally put the bat down, the wooden *thunk* continued as if he were still hitting. Finally, he realized that the sound had nothing to do with a batting cage, and he opened his eyes. When he saw the cabin lit by the morning sun, the previous day came back to him. His heart sank.

Slowly, he got out of bed. The clothes from the day before were laid out on a nearby chair, clean and freshly pressed. The noise that woke him was coming from outside. He got dressed, opened the front door and followed the sound to a small wooded area at the edge of the street.

In a small clearing, a very tall, clean-shaven young man stood over a pile of thick wood pieces which had previously been part of many large branches cut from a fallen tree just behind him. He wore the same kind of shirt, pants, and boots everyone Danny had met wore, and he was the most muscular thin man Danny had ever seen. Even though he was young, his face had a hollow, angular quality set off by a very prominent nose. He held a large axe effortlessly in his left hand, while with his right he picked up a piece of the branch and set it upright on the stump. Suddenly, the axe was in both hands and, after a quick backswing, he brought it down on the log so hard that Danny jumped a little at the force. His hips and shoulders moved in perfect, powerful synchrony to accelerate the axe head to a blur. The log split into even pieces, and he repeated the motion several times without any sign of fatigue. He noticed Danny watching and stopped.

"Good Morning!", he said in the happiest, most contented voice Danny had heard since he arrived. The tall man pointed at the home next to Danny's. It was a small white home with large white columns supporting the front of a shady porch.

"I think we're neighbors. I hope I didn't wake you." He didn't wait to find out whether he had or not before continuing. "I haven't quite come to a conclusion as to what to do with this tree. Every morning I get up and cut it down, and the next morning I get up and it's here again. I do love to swing an axe, and it appears that somebody who knows how to grow a tree has figured that out. I tried to ask the tree about it but…" He paused in an obvious buildup to his big punchline and pointed to the amputated tree base. "We're both stumped!"

Danny forced a polite laugh, but he didn't need to bother. The man laughed for a full minute, and then said: "It feels like I've been waiting an eternity to tell someone that joke. I'm sorry it had to be you." He put down the axe and extended a hand to Danny.

"I'm Abe Lincoln. How do you do?"

The disbelief must have shown in Danny's face. With his hand still out, the man said "Trust me. I'm Abe Lincoln. Nobody else would lend their name to a face like this." He laughed again as he said it.

Danny shook off the feeling of awe and put his hand out. "Danny Boone." For some reason, hi recollection of Abraham Lincoln stayed clear in his mind, while so many other things were blurred.

They shook, and Lincoln said thoughtfully. "Daniel Boone. I think my great-grandfather might have married your cousin." He paused. "But you don't look anything like the pictures I've seen."

"I'm don't think I'm the Daniel Boone you were expecting. I am finally figuring things out. Whatever and wherever this is, they put the wrong Danny Boone here. I have the same name and birthday as Daniel Boone of Kentucky, but I'm a 14 year old boy from Arizona who was hit in the head playing baseball in 2020. I think I fainted when they told me yesterday."

Hearing this, the young man dropped his axe where he stood and stared blankly.

"Is the United States still a union in 2020?"

Danny thought a moment. "Kind of."

"Is Arizona still the same territory as it was in 1863? I recall being very concerned that the Confederacy would take it."

The boy was glad he had paid attention to his state history. "It became a state in 1912."

"And just what do you mean when you say you were hit in the head playing baseball?"

The more they spoke, the more at ease Danny felt. He liked Abe. He was humble, and genuine. He grew more confident, as if he was speaking to a friend in the dugout.

"It's my favorite game and my favorite thing in life. I was playing, and a ball hit me hard in the head and I woke up here. And, judging by the way you swing that axe, you would be a phenomenal hitter. I'm heading into town to pick up some equipment to play. I can come back to get you later, if you'd like to play." The invitation came out so easily, but a small part of Danny's brain couldn't believe he was inviting THE Abraham Lincoln to play baseball.

"Okay", said his new friend. "But before you go, can you answer one last question?"

"Sure", replied Danny, an uneasy feeling growing inside him.

"What happened to me? I remember the war ending on April 9. I remember taking Mary to a play. After that I remember nothing, and nobody here can tell me anything. Most of them can barely remember their own names. For some reason, I can't forget anything."

Danny looked down at the ground, and finally spoke with an uneasy tone. "You were assassinated at the play. Shot from behind. You died the next morning."

President Lincoln looked shocked. "That couldn't happen. John Parker was guarding the door to our box."

Danny shook his head. "He was drinking next door in a saloon."

The color drained from Lincoln's face. An expression of terrible, resigned sadness came to his face. He shook his head and Danny saw tears in his eyes. "My poor, poor Mary. She must have had a terrible time."

Danny nodded. He was sorry he had answered the question; Lincoln had gone in an instant from a laughing young man to a broken man, grieving for his widow. "Please don't be sad," Danny said. " It's the past, and it's over."

"It's never over. The real reason I get up every morning and chop this wood, over and over, staying busy, is to try to shake the feeling that something went wrong. Even 150 years later."

Danny touched his arm. Something about being around this man made him feel smarter and fought the fog gathering in his brain. "We learned about your funeral in school. The train that took you home to Illinois stopped for all people to see you. Every person cried when you went by. At just one stop, three hundred thousand people in Philadelphia waited to pay their respects. Night and day, the tracks were lined with people crying. And Old Bob was there to meet you in Springfield."

"Old Bob was there? He was such a good horse. He was so good with the kids."

"Everyone was there. And you've never been forgotten." He tried to think of a way to cheer him up. "Why don't you come into town with me. I think you're going to like what we find. "

A very slight, sad smile was now on the tall man's face. "I must say, you do have me curious. That's something I haven't felt for a long time." Abe set down the axe, wiped his brow, and set off down the street with Danny.

40

Chapter 6

They chatted comfortably as they walked into town. Abe wrinkled his brow and looked at Danny. "You were talking about playing ball. I used to play ball, but I think it was a little different. You called it baseball. We called it town ball. I used to love to play at Postville Park in Springfield. Sometimes after a tough day in court, the boys and I would play until I was sure that my missus was going to be looking for me."

Danny smiled. "What position did you like to play?"

Abe grinned back. "My favorite was always being the striker, and when my team wasn't at bat, I enjoyed being the fourth basetender. I didn't like much being a thrower, nor did I prefer being one of the scouts in the outfield. I did love to hit that ball, though. My goodness, I loved to hit that ball with the striking stick."

Danny tilted his head toward Abe. "I think you're talking about batters, pitchers, infielders and outfielders. Our striking stick was called a bat. It is used to hit a ball thrown by a pitcher. You'll have to show me how townball worked, but first we need some equipment to play the game."

As they approached the Mayor's office, they saw three large piles of debris in the street. The Mayor stepped into the street and waved hello to Danny, then gestured at the piles. "Here's your stuff, young fellow. All you need to play the game of ball."

Danny looked down at the piles in the street. The first was a stack of broken wagon wheels. Next to that was a large pile of worn and beaten shoes. Finally, closest to the office was a large pile of various colors and sizes of old calfskin gloves. Danny walked over and picked a few up. Some of the gloves were had obviously been worn by working men. They felt flexible but well cushioned. Still, though, he was confused. He looked again at the Mayor, and asked: "Where's my baseball stuff?"

Jacob laughed, but not in a mocking way. "This is your 'baseball stuff'. He looked at Abe. "You've played some ball, Abraham. Would you be so kind as to explain?"

Danny's neighbor picked up a large wagon wheel as if it were paper, and easily snapped a spoke from the wheel. Holding it up to the little group, he said, "This is no longer a wagon spoke. It's a striking stick. You call it a bat. We can shape it a little with some glass filing paper, and it will work just fine."

Danny nodded. "Okay. Where are the balls?"

Abe pointed at the pile of shoes. "Right here. My friend Andy is a tailor and a pretty decent cobbler. In Springfield, before we'd head over to Postville Park to play, we'd have balls made by the same craftsmen."

Just then Danny noticed a smallish man, who appeared quiet and shy, standing just far enough away not to be noticed. The man tried an uneasy grin as he stood.

Abe turned to the man. "Why, it's Andy!". He seemed genuinely surprised. "Hello, Andy! We're glad to see you!"

The man turned red and seemed to physically shrink. "Hello, Abraham", he replied quietly.

Abe turned to Danny. "This is my friend, Andy Johnson. We used to work together."

Andy shook Danny's hand, and nodded in agreement. "I can make the balls", he said. "There's nothing to it. I've seen it done. One melts the sole of the shoes into small rubber balls, and then wraps yarn to bulk it up. You then cut the shoe leather into a pattern of two figure eights and stitch them together."

Danny held up a worker's glove. "What do we do with these?"

Andy took the glove and turned it expertly in his hands. "You'd use this to catch the ball. I can sew material between the fingers to make a net, and put a little padding in. It will work very well."

Abe put his arm around Andy's shoulder. "This is a good man. He'll put it all together for us," he said to Danny. Then he looked at Andy. "Thank you, Andy. It's good to see you again. You need to stop by and visit more often. It's been forever since I've seen you."

Andy looked at the ground for what seemed to be a long time. "I'd like that, Abe. I'd like to talk." He bent over and picked up a large armful of shoes and gloves and started down the street. Danny looked past him and noticed a small hanging sign that read *A. Johnson, Tailor and Shoe Repair.* He could have sworn it wasn't there when they arrived.

"I'll have some balls and gloves ready just past noon", he promised the group.

Danny and Abe walked to the small fountain in the middle of the village. Abe pointed to the bench circling around the fountain. He smiled and patted Danny on the back. "If we're going to play ball this afternoon", he said, "You'd better get up there and try to recruit some players."

Danny looked at the street, which now suddenly seemed much more crowded. "I don't like to talk to groups of people", he pleaded, "Would you please do it?"

Abe gave him another wry smile and raised one eyebrow. "They say once I get started, I might be hard to stop." He climbed up on the bench, and for a moment Danny couldn't see the weeping angel at the top of the fountain.

Danny watched him climb up on the fountain bench. Abe was already tall, and it seemed to make him reach ten feet. Abe cleared his throat.

"Good morning, my friends." When he spoke, he seemed to change. He seemed commanding but friendly, making you want to pay close attention to everything he said Danny squinted at him, trying to figure out what was different. He noticed the square and surrounding streets become eerily quiet, and, as if on cue, the townspeople walked toward the fountain.

Everyone seemed to know who he was and wanted to listen.

Abe was quiet for a moment, and then gave a perfectly sincere smile to the crowd. He leancd toward the group, and said: "There's a boy here who may have been misplaced, and he is missing his home. Now, Mayor Jacob is not at fault, but nevertheless the young fellow is here. And I think he's homesick, and we can all help him to ease his heart a little."

He paused a moment, then continued. "Some of you may or may not know that I used to favor a little game called townball. The boys in Springfield and I would put together a game whenever we could, and it did take your mind off your problems. It's got action, and teamwork, and some pretty healthy ways to enjoy a summer day. Now, Danny plays a newer version of that same game, but I suspect it's improved. We'll need about 20 men and a man who will advise on our techniques of play and keep track of the events of the innings."

He looked out over the crowd and focused on a serious-looking young, African-American man standing with a few other men. The man appeared sturdy and athletic. "How about you Fredrick?"

The man thought for a moment and then nodded. "I'm familiar with the game. My son Charles played for the Washington D.C. Mutuals ball club. I did enjoy the game. I will play as long as you promise not to be upset if I best you in the contest." It was half joking, but half challenging.

"I don't like to lose," replied Lincoln. "But if I do, I will conceal my disappointment and play on. And I suspect that may well happen, given your abilities." Lincoln turned to Danny.

"Please add Mr. Douglass to our team roster."

Fredrick spoke again to Lincoln. "If you're in luck, I may bring a couple of friends to assist in our efforts."

Lincoln nodded to Douglass. "I'm sure that will be very helpful."

Danny's eyes widened. "Fredrick Douglass?" He wrote it down and stared at the man. "Wow. Is there anybody here who isn't a hero?"

It was quiet for another moment, and then a voice came from the back of the crowd. It was a woman's voice, strong and self-assured. "Why are you just looking for men?"

Lincoln paused and reached to rub his chin reflectively while he considered the question. He looked out to the edge of the crowd. Danny wondered if he saw the slightest trace of a smile as Abe searched the crowd.

"Is that you, Martha Jane Cannary?"

The voice added a notable tone of anger. "You know damn well it's me. And you know damn well when you asked for only men that it would get under my hide."

Now Lincoln smiled openly. "You've caught me, Martha Jane. I did indeed leave out our women folk on purpose."

There was yet more anger in the voice. "Why would you do that?"

Abe leaned back a little, and his voice was warm. "Martha, I've seen you ride, I've seen you shoot, and I've seen you handle every tool in this town. I was just hoping to find something you wouldn't show me up at!"

Evidently, this was what passed for humor in town, and as Danny wondered what was so funny that it made the townsfolk convulse with laughter. He stood on his toes and managed to see the woman speaking with Abe. She had long, dark black hair. Her features were sharp, and at first glance she seemed just a little older, maybe a little world-wearier than the rest.

She spoke again. "Well, there's no place in this town you can hide from having to prove you're actually better than me, and not just hiding behind my skirts. William Butler is in, too." She gestured to a tall young man next to her. Danny was surprised to see the man sporting a full, bushy moustache.

Another female voice joined the conversation, this time with a thick southern accent.

"Are you only taking one lady, or may I join in?"

The crowd turned toward the speaker, a tall, fearless-looking African American woman with the sun directly over her shoulder. She was athletically built and spoke confidently. While Lincoln held a hand up to his eyes to see who was speaking, she spoke again. "You don't need to shield your eye to see me, Abe. If I could follow Sherman to the sea I can certainly play this game. Lord knows it does get slow here sometimes."

Danny saw a smile come to Abe's face. "Why, Miss Cathay," he replied, "It would be the greatest pleasure to have you on the team as well. And any others of the gentle sex who wish to compete."

Another woman immediately came back in indignant reply. "Cathay and I will show you gentle when we run you right over!"

The crowd burst into laughter, and Lincoln nodded in appreciation. "Thank you, kindly, Calamity Jane. With this kind of enthusiasm, we're going to have some barnburners. All of you interested, come gather 'round the fountain. We hope to be on the field this afternoon at two. We'll play in the big meadow just north of town." He stepped down from the fountain. The Mayor handed Danny a pencil and paper.

Abe pointed to the list. "Put us down on the list, then add the names of all the folk who spoke up. You can write their proper names, or just note that we have successfully recruited Wild Bill Hickok and Calamity Jane. The second woman was Cathay Williams. She accomplished the undoubtably difficult feat of fighting shoulder-to-shoulder with men in Sherman's Army of the Mississippi as he marched through Georgia to the sea. I have no doubt that both women will add more spice than we might otherwise have expected to our games."

By now, Danny was beyond the point of surprise. He dutifully inscribed the names as Abe had suggested. Napoleon approached him and made a throwing gesture. "I will be your number one thrower, Danny. Arthur and I have been throwing to each other, and he wishes to catch my throws."

Danny dutifully wrote down their names. The two men began to leave, and as they walked away a tall, dark-haired man approached Napoleon. He bowed and said to the shorter man: "*Buenos Dias*, your highness." Somehow, Danny knew he was speaking Spanish, but could again somehow understand every word.

Napoleon laughed. "Hello, Simon, my friend. You always embarrass me when you call me that." He pronounced Simon with a Spanish accent, emphasizing the last syllable.

The man smiled easily. "I saw you crowned King of Italy, my friend. How can I not?"

He turned to Danny. "I want to play your game. I think I will be very good. My name is Simon." He seemed confident but not arrogant. He moved his tall frame with perfect grace. Danny had the feeling he was right about being very good. "I am Simon Bolivar."

While he was getting used to meeting people he had read about, Danny still did a double take. "You are the great general who liberated your entire nation. It is an honor to meet you."

Bolivar paused reflectively and spoke. "Many people liberated our country. I was just lucky to be trusted to lead. How kind of you, though, to pay such a compliment." He bowed again.

"I will see you on the field."

"See you this afternoon," Danny said. Bolivar turned and walked away with long, regal strides.

After watching Bolivar leave, Danny turned around to find a short, somewhat pale young man standing in front of him. He was thin, with the intense kind of pale that resulted more from overwork than laziness. He looked like the kind of person who tended to stay up every night, pushing themselves to study and learn more than anyone else. He had slight rings around his eyes, but spoke with a perfect, crisp clarity.

He extended his hand. "Hello," he said. "I was listening with great interest to Mr. Lincoln. I have since rather hurriedly reviewed material on the game of townball. While I feel I would not play the game well, I have a particular talent for numerical analysis and record-keeping. I have studied the rules and can state that they are indelibly committed to my memory. Prior to my arrival here, I developed machinery that could perform numerical feats heretofore unknown to civilization. Using some rather crude tools, I have constructed the same thing here. I don't know why, but something about this game has struck me as being very amenable to statistical analysis. I would like to apply for the duties of guide and record keeper."

"It sounds like you're talking about a computer,", said Danny.

"My machine certainly computes, but I've never heard that term before. I call it a difference engine. I noticed you looking at the rings around my eyes. Those are from working this previous evening until 4 AM on just that device. And my name", he went on, "Is Charles Babbage."

Danny guessed at the spelling and wrote his name. "Welcome aboard, Coach."

Babbage looked puzzled. "Why would you refer to me as a coach? That is a horse drawn conveyance which has little to do with me."

Danny was beginning to understand more of the gaps in language he was encountering.

"No, no,", he apologized. "I'm sorry. Where I'm from, a coach is a person who steers you to play the game better- like you'd steer a coach."

Surprisingly, Babbage seemed to like the definition. He smiled. "Fine. So it is. I will be a coach to convey improvement in any way possible. May I bring my difference engine to the field to calculate as I observe?"

Danny could only manage a nod. This wasn't exactly going to be the 1988 Dodgers, but he was still excited to get back on the field.

Chapter 7

Several more citizens of the town signed up to play, and soon they had over twenty players, including Danny. Just before two o'clock, the players made their way out to the sunny meadow outside of town. Some rode, some walked, but either way it didn't seem as far to Danny as it had when he arrived. He and Abe both carried their new bats and strolled together, comparing townball to baseball. Abe was shocked that deliberately throwing the ball at the runners was no longer allowed.

"How do you get anybody out?" He asked incredulously.

"You have to tag them," said Danny. Lincoln shook his head. "Too difficult," he said. "You'll be chasing them all over the field."

"No", Danny disagreed, "The have to stay in the basepaths and run from base to base."

"Still sounds like a blindfolded man chasing a fox through the woods to me."

When they got to the meadow, they were happy to see Andrew standing near a large pile of balls and sewn gloves. He walked over to Abe and Danny, handing them each a neatly sewn glove with webbing between the fingers and a comfortably padded palm. Each player's glove fit perfectly.

"My goodness, Andy!", exclaimed Lincoln. "This is a perfect fit. How did you do it?"

Andrew paused a second, then replied quietly. "It's always what I did best, Abe. The other stuff was just not me."

Lincoln put his arm around the man. "Forget the other stuff. Join us. Let's play some ball.!"

The smaller man moved away a bit. "Maybe another time," he said unconvincingly.

Lincoln looked down at him. "I love you, Andrew. A better colleague nobody could want."

The man blushed and walked away. His expression seemed just slightly happier.

The players milled about, trying on their own gloves and beginning to throw balls back and forth. The sun had climbed higher in the sky, and it was starting to get pleasantly warm. Four more men came from the trees into the meadow to speak to Danny. One took the lead. They did not seem to be dressed to play, but nonetheless appeared very interested.

"We heard about your game", the man leading the group said to Danny. He was silent after that.

Danny looked perplexed. "Yes. We're going to be playing some ball. Are you interested in playing?"

"No. We came to visit after considering that a game such as the one you will be playing may have occasional adjudicatory requirements."

"What?", asked Danny.

The man hesitated and then said more slowly, "You may need some volunteers to referee disputes."

"Oh,", said Danny. "You mean some umpires! I didn't even think about that. That would be great!" Thinking further for a second, he asked: "Do you guys have any experience?"

The leader of the group continued to do the talking. "My name is John Marshall. I have extensive experience in resolving disputes, although it has been a long time. Frankly, I miss it. My associates and I would love the chance to involve ourselves in situations that might necessitate arbitration."

"John Marshall? The Chief Justice of the Supreme Court John Marshall?" He thought he was getting used to the unusual people in this town. However, he had to admit to himself that having a Supreme Court Chief Justice as an umpire was, even for this town, pretty exciting. "Sounds great. I have a feeling that with some of the players we have there'll be some pretty big arguments."

He pointed to Marshall. "You stand behind home plate and call the pitches. You are the lead umpire. The other three stand by the bases and make the calls. If the player is safe, you do this."

He crossed his hands and threw them outward. "If they're out, you do this." He put his thumb up and threw his hand over his shoulder. He watched as the four men all tried making the gesture, with varying degrees of success. He smiled watching Marshall instruct the others.

Danny walked to the center of the meadow. He found three small, white sandbags and an iron disc about a foot in diameter. The fact that they hadn't been there a few minutes ago didn't phase him. He was beginning to get used to finding the unexpected. He set the iron disc at a spot that seemed right for home plate, and then paced off the basepaths. The volunteers on the field watched every move and stood looking at the new baseball diamond. After placing the bases, Danny picked up a ball and glove. The ball felt a little softer than those he was used to, but it was nicely sewn and had a nice heft. The glove fit well. It had more padding then he expected and looked comically small. He tossed the ball up a few times and caught it in the glove. It felt good.

He turned and faced the crowd. "Okay", he said. "I know a lot of you have played townball, but today we are going to start learning a different game which I play. It's called baseball. It's closely related but has some important differences."

He noticed the start of many blank looks in the crowd and felt for a moment that he might be losing their attention. He struggled to figure out what to say next. He was nervous. Every person he'd met so far was a legend, and he wasn't sure that the 20th century favorite game of a 14-year-old boy would keep their interest. He looked around. There were women and men of all sizes. Many of those he hadn't met he thought he recognized from pictures in his classes. He decided to speak from the heart.

"Before we get into all the rules, I just want to explain why I love this game so much. And I think when you understand the game, you'll love it at least as much as I do. It's a sport, but it's a science. However, you'll never find a sport with as many numbers and as many players who believe in crazy superstitions no matter what the numbers say." He could see more interest in the players; they were intrigued. He went on.

"I don't know if you have spring here, but where I'm from every year all over the country the snow melts, the grass turns green, and the weather warms up. One day, you go to the closet, and pull out your glove, bat, and ball. You head out to the closest field. There must be something in the weather, since your friends are there. Then you choose teams and play. The first time the ball hits the bat and you run for the base, you feel alive again."

The last part seemed to hit home with the group. They were leaning forward and hanging on every word. From him, the fourteen-year-old who didn't even belong there. He felt much more confident. He looked at Abe, who nodded and raised his eyebrows as if he were impressed.

"Okay." He tossed the ball to Napoleon, who caught it with no trouble and threw it back. "The way we play the game is this: there are nine players on a team. There are also nine innings, and in each inning both teams get a turn at bat…."

Danny gave a detailed outline of the rules and was happy to see people listen intently to all he said. He then asked for two captains to volunteer. Napoleon immediately stepped forward, and they waited for another volunteer. After a minute, a tall, thin but muscular young Japanese man stepped up. Danny held out his hand. "I'm Danny Boone."

The young man bowed politely, and said in Japanese that Danny understood perfectly, "I am Yoshida Shoin." As he spoke, Napoleon leaned toward Danny and said quietly, "The man is a Samurai master. I'm sure he'll be a fine captain."

As they walked to the center of the field, and Danny noticed the difference in how the two men moved. Although shorter, Napoleon had a bold, confident stride which made him appear to be leading a parade. In contrast, Yoshida kept even with Napoleon, but in doing so barely seemed to move. He seemed to flow with effortless balance. Danny could only imagine the kind of warrior he must have been. They reached the center and stood for a moment. After instructions from Danny on how to choose sides, each man picked his team, and the players took the field.

Danny led the two squads in simple drills, working on fielding, throwing, catching, and hitting. After a while, the squads began to play. Napoleon pitched an initial half-inning for his squad. He had a compact pitching style that seem to shoot the ball out of a short barrel at high speed. The first batter was Calamity Jane, who lunged at the initial pitch and almost fell down. Then, appearing more patient, she hit a line drive into right field and easily made it to first before the throw. Once on base, she danced on the bag to distract Napoleon. It seemed like any game Danny had ever played, he thought. Until you considered he was playing with 180-year-old equipment in a strange meadow with dead famous historical figures. Then, maybe it wasn't quite like any other game.

When the bottom of the inning came, Bolivar came out to the mound. Danny had shown him a basic windup, and he had copied those motions and added a few more. It almost seemed that he had created a choreographed dance prior the throw. Danny was surprised to see that his follow-through and accentuation on body mechanics had him throwing faster than Napoleon. The first batters were unable to hit a single pitch. Then Fredrick Douglass came up to bat. Even though Bolivar threw fast, Douglass leaned defiantly into the pitch and hit a fly ball to left center field, which landed between the fielders. He made it to second before the ball came back to the infield. The next batter hit a grounder to first, and Douglass made it to third base easily. He took a long lead, and Bolivar stared at him for a moment. As he began his long windup, Douglass broke for home with short, powerful steps which pushed him to a sprint after a few steps. Bolivar threw the ball too late, and Douglass slid into home headfirst.

"Safe!" John Marshall cried, striking his hands out in to either side, just like Danny taught him.

With his squad cheering wildly, Douglass got up nonchalantly and brushed himself off. The first run had been scored, and Danny couldn't help but be excited. He ran up to Douglass.

"That was fantastic. Who said you could steal home?" He asked.

Frederick Douglass paused for a moment on the walk back to his team's side. He took a moment to catch his breath. He shrugged. "Nobody said I couldn't."

Danny grinned. "Words to live by, Mr. Douglas. I think we've found our leadoff hitter."

Yoshida came up to bat. He held the bat in a high, drawn back posture which made Danny think of holding a sword. The first pitch came, and the samurai swung the bat so hard that many expected the ball to burst as it flew off the bat. He connected easily, and the ball screamed over the heads of the fielders for an easy home run.

Danny's jaw dropped as he watched the man speed around the bases. "We also have at least one power hitter," he mused.

They played until sundown. At dusk, both squads reluctantly picked up the bases and carried their equipment over to the base of the large tree Napoleon had used for practice. They barely got back to town before dark. Danny raised his hand to Napoleon for a high five, but the general gave him a confused stare. "Raise your hand like mine, then we slap our palms together up high. It's called a high five, he explained. It's like a celebratory handshake." The others caught on and tried it, too. After a round of somewhat awkward high fives among the players and officials, they all parted ways and headed home.

Danny and Abe walked together. They were both tired. "It was a great day, thanks to you, Danny," said Abe. "I haven't run so much in years, and being caught in that rundown while trying to get to second base had me panting for breath. Who would have figured that Wild Bill Hickok could be so clever as to fake a throw and then tag me out? I do believe I'll sleep in tomorrow. Maybe I won't get up and cut down that poor tree again, as long as we can play later in the day."

They were almost to their homes. Danny looked at Abe and smiled. "Of course we can play. On one condition."

"What would that condition be?" Abe asked, suddenly sounding like the lawyer he had been before he became president.

"I'm playing tomorrow. Charlie Babbage can coach."

"You're on," said Abe, "just don't block my basepath."

Danny looked at him. "Then stay away from my base."

They both laughed and went inside their homes.

Chapter 8

Danny slept well. The next morning, he woke up very early. There was no chopping noise. There was no noise at all. It was perfectly quiet. He looked out the door. The sky was just beginning to brighten, and the stars were still out. He looked up for a moment but couldn't find any of the constellations he knew. As he put on his fresh clean clothes, he felt as if he had just showered. He was glad of that. Skipping showers and not having to fold clothes was something of a dream come true for any fourteen year-old. He looked past the white columns on Abe's porch to his door. All was still. He suspected that, true to his word, Abe decided to leave the tree alone and sleep. Not wanting to wake him, he took a deep breath of fresh morning air and walked down the street. After a few steps, he caught the delicious smell of fresh bread baking. Suddenly he was hungry. He followed the scent, and after turning a corner to his right, he saw light coming through the windows of a small bakery.

Danny walked toward the lights in the window and read the small sign over the door. There was a loaf of bread hanging by two chains from a small wooden sign embossed with two lines of printing. It read "Patisserie" on the top line; the second line read: "Mssrs. Victor and Alex" in a smaller, cursive print. He knocked softly on the door, and two men came to the door, both reaching for it at the same time. Danny backed up slightly, and both men pulled the thick wooden door open.

Both men stood in the doorway, smiling. "*Bonjour*!" boomed the man on Danny's right enthusiastically. He was a handsome man, and made Danny think of a movie star. His skin was the color of chocolate cream, and his hair dark with dense curls. His voice was deep, warm, and friendly. He continued. "I am Alex, and this is my friend Victor". He spoke French with a strange, antique cadence, but once again, Danny mysteriously understood it perfectly.

"*Bon matin*!" Said the man Alex had called Victor. He was pale, as if he hadn't spent a day in the sun for years, and had black, thick straight hair. He did not sound as friendly, but then reached out and shook his Danny's hand. "You are up early, my friend. I would have thought after all of the sporting excitement yesterday you'd be still in bed!".

News travels fast, thought Danny. He nodded and explained. "I want to get an early start on the day. That was only our first practice, and we have a lot of work to do."

Victor creased his brow, wondering. "Work to do what? You are playing a game in the meadow."

Alex laughed and patted his partner on the back. "Forgive us, monsieur. Victor is always in search of the higher meanings and deeper questions. Sometimes it escapes him that sport in itself can be an object of joy, and improvement adds to that joy. I prefer swordplay with sabers but can understand your dedication to your game of ball. Come in and have breakfast."

Alex and Victor stepped aside to let him in. Danny's jaw dropped when he saw the shelves of bread and pastries the men had baked. Both were obviously very proud. "We present only the best to our fellow citizens," Alex said. That was obviously true. The shelves were full of elegant pastries in all possible different flavors and combinations. Each one was a work of art. There were creme filled eclairs, almond covered croissants, small squares of various cakes, fruit tarts, and more. Victor stepped forward, as if he could not restrain himself. "Which side do you prefer?". At first the question didn't seem to make sense. Then, Danny looked at the shelves again and saw there were actually two counters with a very small space between them in the middle.

He looked at the counters, and at both men. They were watching him, obviously very interested in which counter appeared to have the better pastries. It wasn't hard for Danny to understand that the men, while friendly and apparent business partners, were competing.

He pointed at an éclair in Alex's counter. "May I please have that?" Alex triumphantly walked behind the counter and took a piece of wax paper to grab the pastry. Before he could touch it, though, Danny turned and pointed to a small, round cake in Victor's display case sprinkled with pistachio nuts. "Would it be okay if I also had that cake? These are the most delicious-looking pastries I've ever seen."

The two men looked at each other knowingly. Victor spoke first. "This one is smart. He hardly hesitated before pleasing us both." Alex chimed in. "The wisdom of Solomon, indeed. And so cool while speaking. Impressive grace under pressure." He turned to Danny. "Our young friend. May we offer you an espresso?

Danny thought for a moment about trying one, but then thought the better of it. "No thanks", he admitted sheepishly. "I tried my Mom's coffee once and got sick."

Victor nodded understandingly. "I did as well on my first taste. No need for embarrassment. How about a *chocolate chaud*? We make the best in the universe."

A moment later he placed a large cup of very thick hot chocolate in front of Danny. It had the consistency of cake batter and was incredibly delicious. Danny started to eat and drink slowly. After he had taken a few bites, he looked up and asked the men, "Everyone here seems to be very famous for something. Are the two of you famous?"

Alex paused thoughtfully and then spoke. "Fame is not an accomplishment. Undeserved fame is a mockery of those who have rightfully earned it, and those who triumph in life enough to earn fame don't care whether they have it or not."

"Did you triumph in life?"

Alex smiled. "Our characters did. This seemed to be enough for both us of. However, I would say that the characters of Monsieur Hugo triumphed more than the simple people I devised. His people were full of love, mercy, and great issues; mine were more concerned with running a sword through the right organ."

Victor spoke up. "Monsieur Dumas is far too modest. The people read my books as if they had to. They read his books as if no one could stop them from doing so."

Alex replied a little too quickly, and very pointedly. "But they loved you more, *mon ami*." Danny thought he detected a note of envy in his voice. He spoke up before anything further could be said.

He knew who they were now. "You're both very famous where I am from." He turned to Victor. "I've seen a musical play about one of your books." He noticed Victor give him quizzical look. He continued.

"*Les Miserables*. Monsieur Hugo, the whole world loves it and it never stops being performed." He turned to Alex. "I've seen several stories and productions based on your *Three Musketeers*, Monsieur Dumas. I can't tell you how many swordfights I've had with my friends because of you. They're always the Cardinal's men, and I'm D'Artagnan. I usually win."

Both men relaxed a bit. Victor spoke again. "Solomon, indeed."

Danny cleared his throat. "Do you know what time the bookstore opens?"

Now Alex smiled broadly. "Ah. A young man's dream? You wish to spend time with the sad English poet?"

Danny turned bright red. "No. I just wanted to pick up more books."

Both men laughed. "I hope you are better at your game than you are at lying, my boy,", said Victor. "Nonetheless, good luck. She is a sweet young woman. She has a river of despair which runs through her soul. Take care not to be swept away in that river. Her shop opens in a few minutes."

Danny was still red and couldn't figure out why. He finished his hot chocolate quickly, thanked the two men, and stepped into the street. As he did so, he saw Christina walking to her shop across the street. She saw him and smiled. "A customer! And so early! What brings you here? The last time I saw you, you were passed out on the Mayor's floor."

Danny stumbled for words. "I liked your poems and wondered if you had any more."

She did something of a double take and seemed skeptical. A slight smile played on her lips. As if she were a teacher giving a quiz, she asked the young man. "Which one did you like the best?"

He surprised her by answering without hesitation. "I thought the Goblin Market was good, but a little scary. The two sisters seemed too young to be dealing with goblins."

She nodded, clearly impressed. "I was trying to contrast innocence and evil."

Danny nodded back. "If you say so. It was good, but kind of creepy for me. I hope I'm not offending you."

She smiled a little more. "Not at all. When I wrote it, I knew some would feel that way, but I had no choice. I simply copied it from where it was written on my soul."

Danny wasn't sure why she made him so nervous. "I liked *Echo*. I think my family is sure I'm dead. It made me think of my parents, and how much I miss them. I think of my mother, who's sure I'm gone forever, and wanting me to come back."

She nodded again and recited the first two lines of the poem. "Come back to me in the silence of the night; come in the speaking silence of a dream..." Her voice tapered off.

"It was sad but so beautiful," Danny said. Now Christina turned red. She hesitated, and then spoke quietly. "My life before coming here was not very happy. It always seemed that love and happiness were just around the corner, but when I turned they were lost in the fog. I know I seem sad, but I just can't stop feeling like I should have had just one more chance to find love."

Danny grew bolder. He wanted to say more but wasn't sure what to say. He liked this young woman in a way he'd never felt before and wanted to try to make her smile. "Well," he said, trying to lighten the tone of the conversation. "If you want to see some corners again, come out to the field. We have four of them with a base at each one, and if you want to smile, just watch Calamity Jane try to hit a pitch from Napoleon."

She brightened. "Maybe I will. In the meantime, if you think my goblin poem is scary, try reading this book by my friend Mary." She reached up to a shelf and pulled down a volume.

She handed it to Danny. He read the cover: *Frankenstein, or; the Modern Prometheus*.

"Thanks a lot", he said with some humor. "Now every noise I hear at night will be the monster coming to get me."

She was surprised. "You've read it?"

"Not exactly", replied Danny. "But the story is told a lot. It's very well-known where I live."

"Where is that?"

"Arizona."

"Arid Zone?" She was clearly puzzled.

"No," Danny answered patiently. "Arizona. It's part of the United States. It's in the west."

There was recognition in her voice now. "Yes. The wild west. I used to read dime novels about it when I was ill in England."

"It's still a little wild. Come watch Calamity play. You'll get an idea." He waved goodbye and walked out into the street, carrying his new book. He felt so strange. No sooner had he left than he wanted to return and see her again. He made himself keep walking through the streets, and by the time he got back to his house, Abe was just starting to knock at his door. He saw Danny and glanced at the book title. His brow wrinkled. "Well, that's certainly a cheerful little sunbeam of a book. I don't think I slept for a month after reading it. I kept waiting for that monster to come get me. Quite a change from the Shakespeare I usually read."

"Aren't there witches and ghosts in Macbeth?" Danny countered defensively. "Christina gave me this, and I intend to read it."

Lincoln looked at him knowingly. "Judging from the sound of it, whether there's witches or not around here, you are definitely under someone's spell."

Danny was flustered that Abe had noticed his feelings. "I think I've had enough romantic commentary today. Can we just go play ball?"

"I thought you'd never ask. Put your monster book away, and let's go! And I'll leave you alone about romance. That's a subject which makes fools of us all. Let's leave it to the Frenchmen at the bakery."

Danny agreed wholeheartedly. He opened the door and tossed the book on the table. As he and Abe walked in the direction of the meadow, he started to lecture confidently. "Let me tell you my foolproof way to beat a rundown", he said. "It depends on whether the fielders on both ends have backup when they're throwing." And on he went, until they broke through the clearing to the field and saw a crowd of townspeople playing catch and taking batting practice.

Danny and Abe paused when they broke through the trees and saw the field. It featured an odd-looking crew, all now completely hooked on baseball. The sight of people of all sizes, shapes, and colors wearing 19th century clothing while sprinting after fly balls, diving for line drives, running out grounders, and swinging for the imaginary fence made him smile. This was a capable group of people who were rapidly becoming quite skilled. More people joined as the days went by, and the group was becoming a team. *My team,* thought Danny. *My team.*

Chapter 9

The days passed rapidly, and the game became almost all that mattered to Danny and the other players. When he could forget the pain he felt from missing his family, he found an easy, enjoyable routine to each day. He would get up and put on the clean clothes found each morning in his cabin, and usually walk outside just in time to join Abe walking into town. While Danny never forgot who he was walking with, as time passed, he thought of him less as the man who fought the Civil War and more as his friend from next door with an odd sense of humor. Together, they invariably stopped at the *Patisserie,* where they were boisterously greeted by Alexander and Victor, usually interrupting what appeared to be a spirited argument between the two men. After washing down delicious pastries with coffee for Abe and a hot chocolate for Danny, they'd make their way to the ball field. The field was usually completely full of dust and grime covered players already shouting, laughing, and trash-talking.

On any given day, Danny learned more about his players and their capabilities. One day he watched with surprise as Abe and John Marshall argued for ten minutes over a called strike and had to laugh when the Chief Justice tossed the former President of the United States out of a game. He laughed again when Cathay Williams came up to bat and Calamity Jane shouted in a deafeningly loud voice, "Smack a dinger, Cathay!"

Danny watched with delight as Charlie Babbage became a number-crunching demon of a manager. Anybody arguing with his advice got walked to the difference engine, where they would be promptly buried under an avalanche of averages, statistics, and numerical analysis. After cranking the large contraption of metal poles, counting pieces, and gears, Babbage would come up with inarguable statistics as to why it was bad to steal third when Napoleon was pitching, or who the better fielder was to handle a fly ball between right and center. He also seemed to display of clear sense of baseball intuition. However, when the numbers didn't fit the story, he'd be able to play a hunch or gamble on strategy with the best of them.

As for uniforms, Andrew had made caps for the team just as Danny requested, even embroidering the white "LA" over the medium blue color. The players looked bewildered when Danny explained that those letters stood for Los Angeles. To most of them it meant nothing, but to the puzzled few that knew of Los Angeles it meant that their team was named after a struggling small *pueblo* near the Pacific Ocean.

A typical day's workout included some conditioning drills and light calisthenics, followed by baserunning contests. The team would take batting practice, and then split up for an inter-squad game. Charles Babbage would roam the field, talking to the players and offering tips for improvement. While her preferred playing, Danny remained something of an unofficial coach. He spoke often with Babbage and gave occasional advice. He was surprised to find that coaching was just as much fun as playing. The situations varied from player to player, but there was always advice to give. He watched Oscar Wilde hit a solid line drive. The tall, black-haired man had a nice swing and good eye at bat. However, when he ran past first base and was thrown out trying to stretch the single into a double, Danny tried to offer advice.

"Oscar, why didn't you slide? You had the throw beat, but you came into the base standing up. A hook slide would have put you in for a double."

Wilde looked exasperated. He explained as if talking to a child. "Do you see what I'm wearing?

Danny looked. It was a shirt and pants in the same style as the others. "Yes", he said, not understanding.

Oscar continued, annoyed "Clearly you don't. Every person in this town is wearing cotton or linen. I had to argue with Jacob for years to finally get silk. Now that I have it, I'm not going to ruin these clothes by throwing myself on the ground."

Danny persisted. Now that he was looking, he could see that Wilde's clothing was far grander than the other players. "Yeah, but you hit that so well. It should have been a double. I understand about not wanting to tear your clothes, but you deserved at least two bases after hitting the ball like that. Could you bring a spare pair to the field, so that you might change into fresh clothes if you tear what you are wearing?"

Wilde paused in thought. He looked back at second base as they walked off the field together, and Danny could see he was thinking about it. "I suppose I could", said Oscar. "After all, they're always like new every morning."

"Great!", said Danny. He started to walk away. Oscar tapped his shoulder. "May I ask you something?". Danny could see the look on his face had changed, and he was no longer the confident genius. "Sure", he replied.

Oscar hesitated, almost as if he were scared to speak. The carefree dandy was gone. He was now painfully serious. "It is difficult for many to recall what happened to them before coming here, but not for me. The last part of my life was spent in poverty and suffering, and old friends deserted me. I felt as if I had no one. How am I remembered now?".

Danny brightened. He could answer this. "Well, let me give you an example. My parents took me to Paris last summer, and we walked through a cemetery and saw your tomb. Everyone who walks by kisses it. It's a famous custom, and you're the only person in the world with such a following. The whole thing is covered with the prints of thousands of kisses. At the very least, I'd say people remember you with great affection."

His listener was uncharacteristically quiet for a moment, then Danny saw tears in his eyes.

"That's true?" He asked hopefully.

"How could I make that up?" Danny responded.

Oscar Wilde reached out and put one arm around Danny's shoulders for a moment. "I felt despised, when I had done nothing to earn anger but be myself. Since I arrived here, I've carried that scorn in my heart like a knife wound. Playing ball has been the first thing I've been able to do which lessens the pain, and your words make it all the better. Thank you."

Danny smiled and shrugged. "Just slide into second next time!"

Oscar grinned, just as an intense man with a long beard hit a towering fly ball to left field. He laughed and shouted to the batter who was running somewhat slowly to first. "I say there, Charles! You really hit the Dickens out of that ball. If they throw at you next time you're up, you'd better be an artful dodger." Dickens turned back down the first base line after Wild Bill Hickok made a running catch, and replied somewhat defensively. "I've heard those puns many times, Oscar." Wilde laughed again. "I suppose I do have a bit of a reputation for using the lines of others, but it's too late to reform now." Dickens turned away, with a trace of a smile, feeling he had bested Wilde.

Before leaving Danny, Oscar stopped one last time. "By the way. Christina says to say hello, and hopes you stop to see her again soon." He watched Danny turn red at the mention of her name. He laughed again. "Ah, young love. How exciting. She is very dear to me. Be nice to her."

Danny protested weakly. "I'm nice to everyone."

Oscar winked. "You know what I mean." He looked on the field. "Bolivar is throwing batting practice. I'm going to show him that an Irishman can hit anything he throws!" With that, he walked toward the diamond.

Oscar walked over, picked up a bat, and promptly hit a pitch into the trees. Danny watched and then started on his way back to town. His first stop was the Mayor's office. He knocked politely, and entered when he heard Jacob say: "Come in."

Danny entered. Jacob was sitting at his desk and appeared to be weighing something on a very small set of old-fashioned scales. When he saw Danny, he quickly put the scales into his desk. "Hello, my young friend. How may I help you?"

Danny began. "First, I want to thank you for helping us get a team together. I miss my home, but baseball always helps me to feel better."

"I'm sorry you've been kept here. We haven't been able to locate the Daniel Boone we were expecting, and it's taking time to make arrangements for your departure. We're much better at accommodating arrivals than departures, I'm afraid."

Danny felt the tired, sad feeling that washed over him whenever he thought of his parents and hometown. "I'm grateful to you for working on it. While I'm here, I'd like to ask you for another favor."

Jacob looked wary. "What else?"

"The team has been playing together for longer than I've been able to keep track. It's fun, but getting boring. I'd like us to play another team in a real game."

Jacob sat back with a satisfied nod, as if he had been expecting that question for some time. He leaned forward on his desk. "I think it's an excellent idea."

Danny was surprised. "You do?"

Jacob smiled. "Maybe your coming here was not an error by the universe after all. Since you brought us your game, there has been more excitement around here than I've ever seen. People who previously seemed to be in a helpless daze now spend hours talking about hit and run strategy, or whether an unassisted triple play is possible, or what exactly is the infield fly rule. And they are clearly enthusiastic. It sounds funny to say this, but you've brought the town back to life."

Danny waited and Jacob continued. "I am worried that when you leave, the game may become routine again and our people will drift apart. You have a love for the game which is contagious, and it seems to cement our citizens together. I think playing together as a team against other teams may be helpful to preserve that spirit." He paused and gestured to the doorway. "I'd like you to meet my daughter. I've asked her to help us with arranging a game."

Danny hadn't heard the door open or close, but when he turned around he was startled to see a woman standing behind him. She looked a little older than most of the people in town, but she was clearly younger than her father. She approached him with her hand out and had a beautiful smile. "Hello, Danny. I'm Dinah."

Her dress seemed just the opposite of Jacob's old-fashioned suit. It was long-sleeved and was all elegant ruffles and lace. The only recollection he could match it with was that of a picture of a woman boarding the Titanic in the early 1900's. She wore it in a way that made it seem timelessly classic, and it fit her perfectly.

She continued. "I hear you're a ballplayer."

He collected himself, still surprised by her appearance. He managed to nod politely. "Yes, Ma'am. I love to play."

She smiled again. "Well. I've got a proposition for you. How about a game with the people in my town?"

He was a little confused. "Where is your town?".

"Quite a way from here, I'm afraid. The distance is difficult to explain since it's more a question of time. However, with some planning, I think we should be able to get together."

"Do you have people in your town that play baseball?"

"Indeed. Quite a few. Most of them were born in the late 1800's, but I think it would be best to play the people who played ball in the early 1900's. That way the game will not look quite so different to my team."

Danny hesitated, and then asked, "Are your players dead, too?"

This time it was her turn to be surprised. "Why would you even ask? If you put that question to them, I think they would assert rather forcefully that they are not. Are you dead?"

"I don't think so," said Danny defensively.

"They don't think so either,", said Dinah. "I will admit, though, that even though many have played ball, they have not come together as well as your people. I've scouted some of your practices, and what your players lack in experience they more than make up for with enthusiasm. They seem to love the game."

Danny smiled back. "They all do, but I think it's mainly because we're having fun. I think the secret is that I don't want anyone to feel like it's work."

"Of course not. So, it's settled. We'll plan on playing in about two weeks."

Danny spoke up again before she could continue. "Can I pick the field?"

She thought for a second. "That could be difficult."

He pressed a little. "From what I've seen around here, it should be possible. I want to play the game at Ebbets Field as the home team. The Dodgers played there. I'd like to see it as it was when it was first built. I want the circus seats inside of the left field fence, but I don't want any lights. And I want to try a hot dog there."

"The hot dog may not be quite what you're used to, but I think we can do the rest. You drive a pretty hard bargain. I'm glad we're not trading players. I have a feeling I might come out on the short end."

Danny nodded. "Thank you. I'm looking forward to seeing who's on your team. I had a big collection of books that talk about the history of baseball, and I'd bet that I recognize most of them. But it's not fair that you can scout us, and we can't scout you."

Dinah looked impressed. "That makes sense. What would you propose we do about that?"

"Provide our manager, Charlie Babbage, with the lifetime statistics of each of your players. We'll settle for that."

Now she looked perplexed. "How will that help you?"

Danny smiled. It felt good to have one of the people who appeared to know everything asking him questions for a change.

"Let's just say he's good with numbers."

Dinah gave him a blank look for a moment and shrugged. "Okay. I'll supply him with whatever information you wish."

Jacob stood up and walked over to his daughter. "Good to see you again, Dinah," and gave her a warm hug.

She hugged him back, and then looked at him in a loving but challenging way. "I hope you feel that way when we win."

He rose to the challenge. "Why don't we say a box of our finest French pastries against a large box of fresh Brooklyn bagels. That way when we win, we won't go home hungry and we'll have both."

She laughed. Danny turned for a moment to look at Jacob. When he turned back to Dinah, she was gone. He asked the question anyway. "Two weeks, huh? I guess that means I'll still be here when the game is played, right?"

Jacob was sympathetic. "I think so. But we're working on things. I'm sorry it seems so long."

Danny was disappointed but tried to hide it. "It's okay. We'll work on getting ready. I think everyone will be pretty excited to hear about this." He turned and walked out the door, looking at the ground and already trying to figure out a starting lineup as he walked down the street. Before he could look up, he collided into Christina right outside her shop. She looked just as distracted and surprised as he felt. The armload of books she was carrying tumbled to the ground. As she bent down to pick up the books, she looked up and smiled.

Chapter 10

Danny looked at the scattered books and tried to help Christina pick them up. "I'm sorry," he said. She smiled every more broadly. "Don't be. You've been avoiding me, so it's nice to see you. Even if it did cost me an armload of books."

"I have not been avoiding you," he protested weakly.

"Yes, you have", she said. "I know the signs. Especially when I like the person. I've been through it before. A lot."

Danny figured he'd may as well be honest, even if it made him uncomfortable. "You're right. I'm sorry. I get nervous around you and I don't know what to say."

After he spoke, he noticed something was different about her. She had never looked like this. Previously, she wore dark, dismal clothes and dark makeup. Now, she had a look like springtime. She wore a flowered dress with a light blue and white print. She almost glowed. She appeared happy that he had confessed his nervousness, although he thought he hadn't said much.

"Well, then we're even. I don't know what to say to you, either. But that doesn't mean we shouldn't talk. Part of getting to know each other is figuring out what to say, and the important thing is that we're trying."

This sounded perfectly reasonable to Danny. The more she spoke, the more comfortable he became. He decided to continue speaking from the heart.

"You know," he said. "I'm not very old. I've hardly ever talked to a girl before. That's why I've been so nervous. But I like being around you and I think about you a lot. Does that sound stupid?"

She looked in his eyes. "You're as old as anyone here, and every bit as intelligent and mature. It is perfectly natural, this feeling that grows into love."

When he heard the word *love,* Danny turned bright red. Christina stepped toward him, with an expression of tenderness. She reached up slowly and touched his cheek with her right hand, and she spoke again softly.

"Thank you." She waited a minute and took a breath. "It's been so long since I've touched anyone."

She took her hand away, and then leaned forward and kissed him softly on the cheek. "Don't forget me," she said. "No matter what happens."

Danny flushed again. "I won't forget. You don't have to worry."

Christina thanked him and opened the door to her shop. She turned and smiled again, this time with a trace of sadness. "I know," she said. The door closed behind her.

Danny turned and started down the street. The pastry shop was on his right, and as he walked by the door opened. Victor motioned him into the shop and handed him an éclair. "*Tres bien*, my young friend. With your love, the sad poet is blossoming like a rose."

"Were you spying on me?" Danny demanded.

"That's a very harsh way to put it," replied Alexander. "We were just working and couldn't help but notice your interaction. We are grateful for it. Forever she has been a black cloud to share a street with, but because of your love she is now a ray of sunshine."

"Love?" Danny said incredulously. "I'm only fourteen."

Both men smiled. "Not anymore, *mon ami*", said Victor sympathetically. "You are now as old as the oldest of us. Love is what makes a man."

Danny left, munching on the éclair as he walked off. He found all of this talk of love exhausting. He wanted to get away and return to what he knew–baseball. He walked quickly to the town square, and saw Napoleon at the fountain, tossing a ball into the air and catching it with his glove. He was discussing catcher's signals with Bolivar. "One finger should always be a fastball," he argued. "It's the most common pitch."

Bolivar replied with equal intensity. "All the more reason, *amigo*, to make the signs more *complicado*. If they steal your signs, you need to make it difficult."

Napoleon sighed. "I don't know if you need more than one sign, *General*. I think only one of us can throw a curveball, and I'm not sure that either of us has more pitches than that."

Danny joined the conversation immediately, happy to talk about anything else. "Where I'm from, there's a pitch called a screwball. Also, a knuckleball. There's also one called a changeup. And there's more."

Both men turned and looked at Danny. Bolivar raised an eyebrow and leaned in to speak with him. "Exactly when were you going to tell us about these pitches? Sometime in the ninth inning of a tied game?"

Danny shrugged. "A fastball and a curve are all most great pitchers throw. And once they're used to the speed, you just throw a slow one. That's a changeup. We'll learn the rest when we play the team from the 1900's."

Napoleon started to say something, and then did a double take. "What did you say? The 1900's?"

Danny explained about the meeting with Jacob and Dinah, and the game that was coming up in two weeks' time. Both became wide-eyed. Napoleon began to talk rapidly, with excitement. "We will easily defeat the future men. I'm sure that they are soft and not at all like the strong men we are."

Bolivar laughed. "My emperor has already played the game in his mind. He was always the brilliant strategist. But don't forget, they are just men and women, and we also have the secret weapon of Miss Calamity. How can we lose?"

Danny frowned. "Actually, there are a million ways we can still lose. Just ask the 2019 Houston Astros."

Together, they looked at Danny. "Neither of those words make sense," said Napoleon.

"They were famous for stealing signs," said Danny. "Sign-stealing doesn't make any sense to me. It's just not sportsmanlike. It was especially painful if you were a Dodger fan."

Bolivar clapped his hand around Danny's shoulders. "*Jefe*. After all you've taught us, you apparently don't understand a basic fact. We're all joyous believers of your

Dodgers of the little pueblo of Los Angeles, even if we have no way to know that they actually exist. When I pitch, I am thinking about the great Kershaw and hoping I may throw as well as he does."

"Well," said Danny, putting the Astros out of his mind. "Let's go tell the rest of the team about the big game. We've got a lot of work to do."

The three of them left the fountain and turned to the road toward the playing field. As they walked, Danny stole a glance back down the street, and saw Christina leaning against the door of her shop, watching him. She smiled and gave a small wave. Danny waved back and wondered at how such a small exchange could make him so happy.

When they got to the field, Danny saw Abe hitting towering fly balls to a small group of players. He squinted into the afternoon sun and could barely make out Yoshida and two other men whom Danny believed were being taught the way of the samurai. They centered gracefully under each ball, easily catching them all and dropping none. After every catch, Danny could hear the soft encouragement and teaching of their instructor. Each played as if they instinctively knew the right moves to make to move perfectly and allow each ball to find its home in their glove.

He walked up to Abe. "Those guys move so smoothly. They make it look so easy. They look like they were born to play the game."

Abe hit another high fly and watched in admiration as they ran it down. "I could not agree more. And, I am embarrassed to say that prior to our adventures out here on the field, I had no idea of the extent of their skills and philosophy. I must complement you on bringing this game to us. It's not only challenging and lends itself well to thought and analysis, but also seems to promote friendship among those playing."

Danny shrugged his shoulders. "Where I'm from, we call it having fun."

Lincoln nodded. "It certainly is that. You look a bit flushed. Have you been spending time at the bookshop again?"

Danny sighed loudly. "Is there anything private in this town?"

"There might have been for the first one hundred or so years", replied Abe. "But we are all so happy to see you bring some cheer into that young lady's life. I don't know all the details, but from what I've heard she had a rough go of it before coming here, and never found love."

Danny gritted his teeth. "You sound like one of the books by Victor and Alexander. Love. It's all they can talk about."

"I have read more than a few." Abe spoke gently. "I'm sorry to pry into your affairs. All of us are grateful you're here, and there seems to be no limit to the joy you've brought to our town. I miss my Mary so much, and most of us found love prior to coming here in one way or another. That young lady seems to have missed so much in life, and you appear to be changing her whole person just by kindness and affection."

"Do you mind if I change the subject?" He felt more than a little uncomfortable and was relieved when Abe agreed. "I have a big announcement to make." Danny whistled loudly to call everyone together. The team stopped playing and slowly gathered around. He called Charles Babbage to the center and whispered in his ear for a moment. Babbage raised an eyebrow and whispered a few questions back to Danny. Then, he held up his hands and asked for silence.

"Our young friend brings us exciting news. We have a game arranged with a team from another town. We play in two weeks."

Calamity Jane pushed to the front. She was clearly excited to compete. "Just who are these people?"

Babbage replied. "Apparently these are ballplayers from a time after ours. They've all been born in the 19th century, but played in the 20th. They will be skilled, and many of them played ball as a vocation."

Jane laughed out loud. "They got paid for playing baseball? You've got to be joking!" She looked at Danny. "Why would you get money for doing something that's fun?"

Danny found it harder to explain than he thought it would be. "In my time, the skills of the players and a person's loyalty to teams representing a city created a demand to see the games. There were beautiful stadiums which held thousands of people, and it was a great way to spend time."

Oscar Wilde raised his hand. "A stadium? Like the Colosseum of ancient Rome?"

"Close," admitted Danny. "But nobody gets eaten or killed. And if there's any fights, they usually don't amount to much. I've asked that we play in a stadium which I've never been to, but I've heard was legendary before it's destruction. It was called Ebbets Field, and was in Brooklyn."

This provoked a roar of laughter from the residents who hailed from America. A structure comparable to the Roman Colosseum in New York city? Players were paid to play there with thousands in attendance?

Oscar continued. "I've been to Brooklyn. I'm not sure I could be paid enough to play there."

Danny started to become very defensive, but before he could speak Wild Bill Hickok cut him off and addressed the group. "Don't laugh at what you don't understand. This young man has the advantage of knowing many things we don't. I say we go to Ebbets Field, and we whip the tar out of whoever we play!"

This brought a loud cheer from the crowd. Charlie Babbage stepped forward.

"We're going to be practicing very hard over the next two weeks. I'll be doing a lot of analysis to determine what positions will be assigned and who will be our starting nine players. Some of you may be better suited to having more playing time in order to attempt to secure victory. I hope that does not offend anyone." No one seemed to be upset.

Charlie stepped over to his difference engine and picked up a clipboard. "I've done some preliminary analysis." He turned to Fredrick Douglass. "Mr. Douglass. You successfully reach first base far more than anyone else here when you bat. That is an extremely valuable skill, and I think by far qualifies you to hit in the first position. Are you amenable to that?

Douglass smiled modestly. "Of course." His friends each gave him a congratulatory pat on the back.

Babbage continued to discuss positions in the batting order. When he finished, the lineup had Douglass batting first and playing third base. In the second position and also playing second base was Danny. Yoshida Shoin played left field and was batting third. Batting fourth and playing first base was Abe, who seemed to never let a hittable pitch go by. Oscar Wilde was playing center field and hitting fifth. Calamity Jane was in right field, and under protest agreed to bat sixth. Arthur Wellington had proven to be great catcher with a formidable throwing arm, and hit seventh. Hitting eighth and playing shortstop was Charles Dickens, who had proved to be an intensely focused fielder who would stop a ball by any means possible. He also had a steady output of opposite field line drives when hitting. Finally, Napoleon was named as the starting pitcher and hit ninth.

This group played together on the field as much as possible, and the opposing squads tried hard to beat them. Danny was everywhere helping the other players, and his enthusiasm was infectious. Soon the whole group was playing hard as a unit, and the daily progress was impressive.

Finally, it was the day before the game. Danny hadn't spent as much time with Christina as he had wanted, and on the way home tried to walk by the bookstore. Just before he reached her store, the door to the Mayor's office swung open. Jacob looked out and called to him. Danny stepped into his office. Jacob was obviously excited.

"Great news!", he said. "Things have finally aligned. You'll be able to return home soon. I can't say exactly how, but it will happen."

Danny was surprised that the news did not make him as happy as he had expected. He thought about it quickly, and then suddenly understood what was bothering him.

"No."

Jacob was clearly taken aback. "No? I thought this was what you wished for?"

Danny was quiet for a moment. He was nervous, and not sure how he could say it. "It was at first. But now, I have friends here. And I don't want to leave Christina."

"Ah," Jacob said knowingly. "The talk of the town is correct. You are in love with her."

While he was getting used to the gossip, it still made him turn red. "I don't know about that, but I do care a lot about her. She got a bad deal in her life, and I want things to be better for her."

The Mayor looked confused. "How can I affect that? She's here, and I can do nothing for her life prior to this."

Danny stood firm. "From what I've seen, there's a lot you can do if you decide you want to. You owe me. I was brought here by mistake, and I haven't complained. I think I've been a good sport about it. If I go, I want her to have a chance somehow to find happiness- even if it's not with me. I don't want her to be sad anymore. She deserves a chance to have someone love her and to love her back. If you can't do that, I'm not going."

"Impressive negotiating skills for a fourteen-year-old who fainted the first time he was in my office," said Jacob. "You are correct in that we made an error. And yes, we are grateful for your presence here. I can promise you that I will do my best to provide her with an opportunity to find love again, but I'm afraid I don't know how just yet."

Hearing that made Danny feel a mix of being happy and sad. He thanked the Mayor and left the office. Next door, Christina was just closing up the bookshop. She smiled when he opened the door and stepped in.

"Everybody's talking about the big game tomorrow," she said. "I hope to attend."

"I hope you can, too." He drew upon all of his courage, and then said, "I've never known anyone like you before. As much as I like baseball, when I see you, nothing else is seems as important."

She beamed at him and took his hand in hers. "I feel the same way, and it seems that there has never been a time in my life when I didn't know you." She started to say more, but before she could Danny stepped forward and kissed her lightly. He was very tentative, and after he drew back, he didn't know what to say. "Was that okay?", he asked.

"Oh yes", she said. "I've been waiting every day for you to do that." She reached out, took his hand and gave it a gentle squeeze. "You have a big day coming up. Please rest, and I'll be watching your team win tomorrow."

He felt his heart pound. "Okay", he said. "I'll be looking for you."

"And I for you."

He walked out the door and headed for home. As he passed the pastry shop, Victor winked at him through the window. Danny wanted to be offended, but could not stop himself from smiling back.

He slept soundly that night, dreaming about seeing Ebbets
Field in the morning. When he woke up, he felt ready to play.

Chapter 11

The whole town was buzzing with excitement. At the pastry shop, Alexander and Victor chattered enthusiastically about the big game. They were confident their team would be victorious. As they left the shop, Victor shouted: "To the barricades!" Alexander rejoined with: "All for one, and one for all!" Outside, the weather was even more perfect than usual. Danny's stomach fluttered with the familiar nervous anticipation of a big. He caught up with Abe, and they joined Napoleon and Arthur at the fountain of the weeping angel.

They began down the road to the field, and Danny looked around the group. He noticed that while he was nervous, everyone else seemed perfectly nonchalant.

"Are you guys nervous?", he asked before confessing. "I am."

The three men looked at him. All smiled.

Arthur replied first.

"Are you asking if we want to win the game?"

"I guess so."

Napoleon patted him on the back. "*Mon frere,*" he reassured Danny. "Nervous for us is when you are being charged by a massive army being led by this man." He pointed to Arthur. "And you realize that you are going to be beaten, maybe killed, and all of those who believed in you will suffer."

Arthur nodded. "Or when you are attacking the greatest general who ever lived."

Napoleon smiled at this and continued. "But we learn from such times in life. This is an important day. It is a day to celebrate and enjoy. We get to play a game we now love against some of the greatest players ever, thanks to you. I was throwing rocks at trees before we met. Now I stare down the batter and aim for the outside corner to strike them out."

He kept talking. "Besides playing the game itself, I feel blessed to have become part of a team with so many that I did not know well before, but now would do anything for. The other day, Cathay hit my best pitch over the center fielder's head, and while I wanted to be angry, I couldn't help but cheer her when she slid into third. That is what it feels like to be on a team."

Abe continued down the road in silence for a moment, then spoke in his now-familiar quietly thoughtful way. "I like that you're feeling some nerves, Danny. It means that you feel a challenge is ahead, and you have the chance to prove to yourself that you are the equal and better of it. I suspect you'll face many such challenges, but as your friend, I know you will always come out on top."

All were quiet for a moment. Then Abe spoke again.

"When I lived in Springfield, I had a friend named Billy. He was loyal, honest, and one of the finest people I've ever met. I miss him greatly but meeting you and playing this game of yours has reminded me of just how good it is to have a friend. I believe the whole town feels that way about you, and we're glad you wandered into our lives. So, if you're nervous, just remember that every person on this team is grateful to you and will give everything they've got to win. I think you'll find that we know a thing or two about winning."

When Abe finished, Arthur moved over and put his arm around Danny's shoulder.

"What he means, young chap", Arthur said with an impeccable British accent, "Is that you have changed our lives by teaching us to be a team. Plus, I think you've introduced me to a game I like more than cricket."

As he finished, they stepped onto the short path through the forest. The roar of a crowd rushed at them from a distance. Danny's heart leaped. It wasn't the noise of any crowd. It was the noise of a ball game. An organ began to play, and he could make out the sound of vendors calling out their familiar refrain: "Peanuts! Popcorn!" It reminded him of when he was a young boy going to Dodger stadium for the first time. Their little group broke through the trees into the clearing, and Danny's jaw dropped.

The meadow was no longer a meadow. Inexplicably, a massive stadium with a marble roof over the entrance and beautiful framed windows allowing streams of brilliant sunlight now stood in front of them. The building stretched across the meadow, but not enough to stop the thousands of people streaming in from their side and the other side of the meadow to enter the stadium. It was spectacular. Danny had to stop and stare. Large letters stood at the top of the rounded front of the building, spelling "EBBETS FIELD".

He was dumbfounded. After a minute, he said to nobody in particular, "I was half joking. I didn't think we'd actually get Ebbets Field." He looked the building over again. It was beautifully designed, and the marble reflected the midday sun like a giant mirror. He felt a twinge of envy, a little jealous of the fans who got to watch the Dodgers there for so many years. He loved Dodger stadium, but this seemed so beautiful and somehow made him feel more like he was closer to home.

Danny looked at Abe, Napoleon, and Arthur. They were also staring, but clearly not understanding what they were looking at.

"We call it a ballpark," Danny explained. "If you think it's pretty on the outside, wait until you see the inside." With that, he led the four of them through the crowd to the entrance. People were pouring in through turnstiles in the front. There were no ticket takers, but men in uniforms resembling railroad conductors were watching the crowd. As

Danny and his group approached the turnstile, the attendant leaned forward and stopped his entrance.

"You need to go through the player's entrance", he said curtly, gesturing with his head to his right. Danny turned, and noticed a door with another attendant standing guard. **HOME TEAM**, it read in block printing on the door. He looked across the entryway to the other side, and saw another door labeled **VISITING TEAM.**

Just as he looked the opposite door opened and another young man stepped out looked over at him. The man stood almost a full head taller than the crowd, He looked more like a boxer than a baseball player. He wore a three-piece suit with a high, white starched collar and a straw hat. When he saw Danny, who was wearing his usual loose fitting linen shirt, with baggy pants tucked into his boots he smiled and shook his head. Danny stopped, and stared back at the man without smiling. With this, the other man's face reddened with apparent anger. Danny held the door, not moving, and looked at him with no expression. He'd had other players try to stare him down and intimidate him before, and he wasn't going to let it happen here. The other man, clearly expecting a different response, slammed the door without entering and pushed through the crowd with his hat off. When he got to the Home Team door, he pushed his face closely to Danny's. He appeared full of rage. Danny wasn't scared; in fact, he was pleased that he appeared to be the same height and weight of the large young man. He leaned in and stared back.

The man in the suit started to speak. Danny could smell tobacco on his breath, and he noticed stains from chewing on his teeth. Before he could get a word out, Danny spoke.

"Hello, Frank."

This startled the man. "How do you know my name? Is this some kind of cheat?"

Danny smiled and turned to Abe, Napoleon, and Arthur.

"This is Frank Chance. He's the first baseman of the opposing team. He may be the greatest first baseman to ever play the game. He played for the Cubs when they won the World Series in 1907 and 1908. He'll probably be helping to manage the team as well."

Hearing this, Chance relaxed a little but remained mildly threatening. Danny continued.

"The problem is, he had a pretty bad temper. He was the first player to ever be thrown out of a World Series game. Some people said that he made Ty Cobb look like a perfect gentleman. He swore and fought his way through the game like nobody else. He threw bottles at the crowd in Brooklyn. He was hit in the head so many times by opposing pitchers that he needed brain surgery." Danny looked at the side of his head and nodded.

"Yup. You can still see the scars."

Now Chance reverted back to sheer anger. His face reddened. He started to step toward Danny. Suddenly, Abe stepped between them. His 6'4" height made the other man look small, and Abe appeared friendly but fearless. He laid a hand with an iron grip on Chance's shoulder.

"Hello, Frank. I'm Abe. Why don't you just take a step back? We don't want to start any ruckus before our game is even played, do we?" He said this while looking directly into his eyes.

The angry man appeared to ponder this for a moment. He looked at Lincoln's height, his sinewy arms, and sensed the strength the man had. He stepped back. He looked up at Lincoln, then over at Napoleon and Wellington. He turned, spat a large glob of tobacco on the ground, and then snorted.

"I know who all of you are and I don't care. You fancy boys shouldn't even be sharing the same field with my team. We're going to cut you to pieces."

Napoleon laughed with delight, which clearly was not the reaction Chance expected. He looked bewildered for a moment, then scowled. Napoleon squinted one eye and looked at him.

"Monsieur. How nice of you to issue such a challenge. It makes things so simple and provides motivation. But may I make a suggestion? You might not want to directly threaten the man who will be pitching the ball your way. I suspect that may be how you obtained such scars on the head." He smiled when he finished.

Chance started to spit again, then stopped. "Do your worst", he said. I'll hit anything you throw."

Napoleon grinned again. "I look forward to it, *mon ami*." While Chance stood glaring, the four men turned away and entered the Home Team door.

Inside the short hallway, Danny could smell the leather of the gloves and balls, and he could hear a light, bouncy tune from the organ coming through the walls. He turned to Lincoln. "This was the first ballpark to have a full-time organist." Abe listened to the pleasant music for a moment and smiled. "They'd better be careful, or they'll have to see me dance!"

They came to two doors, separately labeled. "Gentlemen" and "Ladies". He knocked on the Ladies door.

It swung open immediately, and Jane answered. "Why are Cathay and I stuck in here by ourselves? We both fought in the Indian wars. Do you think you men have anything we haven't seen before?" Cathay stepped up behind her and added, "I fought in the regular army for years. I don't like being apart from the team."

Lincoln spoke diplomatically from behind Danny. "We don't mean to separate you two from the team. It's just some of the men may be a little shy to have a lady watching them change their britches. We'll have you in with us in a just a wink."

They went through the other door and walked into the rest of the team getting dressed. The locker room smelled like home to Danny. There was a strong fragrance of freshly oiled leather gloves, the smell of pine tar on bats and the fragrance of fresh uniforms. When he saw the uniforms Andrew made, he smiled. He had shown him how the word "Dodgers" was written in cursive, and how the tail of the last letter swung back to underline the name. It was scrawled perfectly across the front of each jersey, and on the back was the last name of each player over the number they selected. Danny had picked 13. It had always been unlucky for everyone else but him.

Wild Bill walked over to Danny, holding a jersey and looking at it quizzically. He wore no shirt, and Danny noticed

Jane looking through the door, watching every move Bill made. "Why are we called the Dodgers?", he asked Danny.

"It's my favorite team, and I agreed to play on the condition we could wear the uniforms. They began in Brooklyn, where people used to have to dodge the trolley cars going through the streets."

Hickok smiled. "That's rich. I've dodged a few things myself," glancing briefly at Jane. "I'm proud to wear the colors."

Danny picked up his jersey, which sat beside a fairly modern looking pair of cleats and stockings. Once everyone was dressed, Jane and Cathay formally joined them. He demonstrated how to put on and wear the cleats. They felt much more comfortable than the boots he had been wearing, and the rest of the team appeared to appreciate them as well. When they all had shoes on, Charles Babbage walked to the center of the room, carrying an armload of small folders filled with papers. He cleared his throat.

"I know you are all as excited as I am. We've worked hard to develop our skills to the point where I think we can challenge this team and win."

He held up the folders. "Using my difference engine, I've compiled a large number of statistics on each player on the team. These are experienced players who were outstanding when they played. However, they were not perfect, and I think each has weaknesses in their play we may capitalize on to our advantage. I will refer to this information throughout the contest."

Oscar Wilde held up his hand. "What kind of information might help us, Charlie?" He appeared, like the rest, to be a little nervous about playing an unknown team.

Charlie looked down at the folders and pulled the first one off the top. He opened it and began to read.

"One such file is on their center fielder. He's a boy from Georgia, and quite a player. Apparently, he set over 90 records when he played ball, and was an almost perfect player. However, the numbers show that he did not always throw well from the outfield. Therefore, if there is a runner on first and the ball is hit to him, we may attempt to reach third instead of second."

"What is his name?", Oscar asked.

"Ty Cobb,", answered Danny. "He plays fierce and hard. Be careful if he is coming at your base. He'll slide high and try to catch you with his cleats."

He paused for a second. "What is their starting lineup?"

Charlie pulled out a list.

"Let's see. Their starting pitcher is a right-handed pitcher who goes by the nickname of Smoky Joe Wood." He looked up at Danny. "He seems to be very proficient and have a high velocity when he pitches the ball to the batter."

Danny nodded. "People say that he might have been the fastest pitcher who ever played. It may be intimidating, but remember this: when they throw hard, if you can get a bat on it, the ball will go much farther."

Charlie nodded. "Very good point. Newton's third law. One only needs to connect." He looked at the paper. They have only listed one other player. A young man who played on the same team—the Boston Red Sox—as Mr. Wood. His name was George Ruth. He throws left-handed."

Danny took a step back, clearly struck by this. "Wow," he marveled. "The Babe."

Fredrick Douglass asked quizzically. "He's an infant?"

"No," explained Danny. "He was signed to the Red Sox when he was very young, so he was called 'Babe' as a nickname. He was a strong left-handed pitcher, but later became an even better hitter."

Douglass looked less puzzled, but still shook his head. "I think I would prefer a nickname which would not refer to a small infant."

Charles Babbage continued.

"They are being managed by a man named John McGraw. He looked at Napoleon. "He has impressive statistics for winning, but is also troubled with something of a volatile temper. He also has been cited historically for attempting to circumvent the rules to gain advantage in a contest."

Yoshida Shoin appeared confused by this. "Why would one compete and not play fairly? That would defeat the purpose of a contest. It would bring dishonor to the entire team."

Danny tried to explain. "For some people, winning is very important, even if they don't play the game fairly. I'm not sure how things got that way over time, but it happened. We'll have to watch for any suspicious play. Where I come from, a team called the Astros won championships and were cheating the whole time. In my time, there was no real punishment and no one seemed to care."

The Samurai was mystified. "I cannot understand how such people could play dishonorably."

"It happens", said Danny. "But we won't."

Babbage looked again at the paper.

"The infield is Heinie Groh at third, Honus Wagner at shortstop, Napoleon Lajoie at second, and Frank Chance at first. I hear you've met Frank Chance."

Abe waved his hand dismissively. "That young man's not aware that he's looking for more trouble than he can poke a stick at. Let's just see if we can keep it to playing ball with him."

Charlie continued. "Connie Mack is catching and," he paused and looked at the paper, "Tris Speaker is in left field. He was a pro ball player back in his day. He has amazingly good numbers and would usually play center field. A player named Wahoo Sam Crawford is in right field. He is a superior player, but is also a strong rival to Ty Cobb. They both played for the same team and constantly competed."

Babbage put the folders back under his arm. "There are many statistical aspects of this team to measure, but the most important thing may be something that cannot be measured. We have a team: a group of players who may have been strangers and rivals in some other life, but now care more about each other than themselves. Our opponents were all great players, but it may be hard for them to sacrifice for the others because of lapses in character. To our credit and advantage, every one of you is a great person, and together you make a strong team." He flushed with embarrassment, thinking he had displayed too much emotion. "Godspeed to us all, and most of all, enjoy the game. Games, after all, were meant to be fun."

He turned and walked toward the back of the clubhouse, and out toward the tunnel that led to the field. Danny followed, and as his cleats echoed down the hall, the crowd grew louder.

Chapter 12

The end of the tunnel to the field was lit with the bright sun. Danny reached the stairs and walked to the top alongside Charles Dickens. Danny and Dickens saw the field at the same time and gasped together in unison. The ballpark was more beautiful than Danny dreamed. He had played on many diamonds and seen games at many major league parks, but nothing he'd seen came close to what he encountered walking out of the tunnel at Ebbets Field.

He stood for a minute. A soft breeze blew around him. It was all perfect. Every blade of grass seemed in place, the infield lines were crisp and sharp, and it seemed every seat was taken. The same breeze ruffled a long row of flags, flying on short poles ringing the stadium. Danny couldn't count all of them, and stopped trying after finding the American flag, the Union Jack, the French Tricolor, and the Bolivian flag with the beautiful coat of arms. The whole view was breathtaking and beautiful, like all great ballparks, in a timeless way.

Danny glanced around the stands. Behind the plate and down the third base line he saw the citizens of his town. They were distinctive in their 19th century clothing, and he recognized most of their faces. He couldn't stop himself from looking, but didn't see Christina among them. On the first base side, a large contingent of men and women were dressed in the fashion of the early 20th century. There were a few people he thought he recognized: a man who looked like Theodore Roosevelt, pointing, gesturing, and explaining things to anyone who would listen. A man with dark hair and a serious look sat next to him; he wore the uniform of a World War I U.S. Army soldier with a small pair of wings over the left breast pocket. On his other side sat a stylishly beautiful young woman, wearing a perfectly matched dress and hat. She was politely tolerating the stares and double takes of men around her, dumbstruck by her beauty.

As Jacob, the Mayor, approached them, Danny looked at the crowd farther down right field line. That area was isolated from the rest of the stadium by shadows and darkness. It was hard to make out any one person. The crowd seemed a mess of featureless faces with glowing red eyes. A dark gulf separated their section from the rest of the spectators. A low growl and humming noise appeared to emanate from that area, but he couldn't be sure exactly where it came from. Even though it was mid-day, the shadows of the section would have small tongues of flame randomly appear for a moment, then disappear. Though he couldn't comprehend what he was seeing, the sight filled Danny with fear.

Jacob stepped behind Danny and Charles Dickens, noticing the focus of their attention.

"Just ignore the right field crowd," he said in calming manner. "That's Dinah's doing. She's apparently quite serious about winning and had to make a deal to bring Cobb and Chance here. Those are fellow citizens of the particular town Cobb inhabits. It's best not to dwell on it."

In front of that area of the grandstand was a small man in a modern suit, in the act of lighting a cigarette with what appeared to be his hand. "That's their mayor. His name is Applegate. Don't listen to anything he has to say, whatever you do."

Watching him in front of the odd forms and flickering flames in the grandstand gave Danny a sick feeling, which disappeared when he looked away. "That won't be hard," he said to Jacob. "He gives me the creeps."

"He should", said Jacob. "Steer clear of him. He owns the soul of everyone behind him."

They watched as the home plate umpire, John Marshall, walked toward the mound. A large, extremely heavy man wearing umpire gear walked alongside him, and as he began to wave to the crowd, Danny could see Roosevelt stand up and boo him so loudly that it echoed through the entire stadium.

Charles Babbage and John McGraw each approached the mound, Babbage acting as if he'd done it thousands of times in the past. They exchanged a few words, handed a list with their starting lineup to Marshall, and walked back to the sidelines. The Dodgers walked into their dugout and marveled at the water fountain until Babbage sharply directed their focus to the game again.

The teams were called to stand on the foul lines by the announcer, who introduced himself as Gabriel. As they stood, music played that Danny recognized as *The Star-Spangled Banner*. As he looked up and down the baseline, he saw tears stream down the faces of Napoleon, Wellington, Bolivar, and most of the other players. He realized that they were hearing their own anthems. Watching them made him realize how much their own countries meant to them. He looked down the row of players to his left and saw Lincoln's face glistening with tears. The tall man appeared to be simultaneously choking back grief and beaming with pride at the same time, and the sight of it made Danny stand even taller.

When the anthems ended, he heard Marshal shout, "Play ball!" The Dodgers were the home team and ran out to the field. Napoleon and Wellington set up on the mound and home plate, and started some warmup throws. The infield

Babbage had chosen started throwing to each other. Lincoln was at first, Danny at second, Dickens at shortstop, and Douglas at third. In left field, Oscar Wilde was taking throws from Yoshida Shoin in center and Calamity Jane in right. After several minutes John Marshall stepped out in front of home plate and called for the balls to come in.

Lincoln and Jane tossed the balls to the right field line. Abe tossed one ball underhand to the young man in an Army uniform next to Roosevelt. The brass wings over his left pocket glinted in the sun as he reached for the ball. He caught it with his left hand, and at the same time saluted Lincoln with his right. Roosevelt watched the interaction between the two with a smile that also showed sadness. He smiled and nodded a thank you to Lincoln.

Farther down the right field line, Calamity walked over toward the grandstand and stared at the writhing mass of odd shaped forms crowded together, noticing occasional glowing red eyes try to focus on her. Trying to suppress a feeling of dread, she tossed the ball into the stands. A hole appeared in the middle of the crowd, with a fiery glow deep at the base. The ball went directly into the center of the hole, which then closed immediately. Just before it closed, Jane thought she heard a sound which sounded like a cross between a moan and a scream. She turned to walk away and saw Applegate. He looked back at her and beckoned with a smile. She shuddered, turned away, and jogged back to right field.

Napoleon watched as Wellington made a perfect throw to second, and then took the ball back from Danny. Heinie Groh was in the on deck circle and walked to the plate. He had his trademark "bottle bat", with the handle cut down abruptly to resemble an inverted soda bottle.

Groh stepped into the right-handed batter's box and stared at Napoleon. He looked at Napoleon and spoke to him in a low voice.

"Frenchie. This is a man's game, and you are no bigger than a boy. Be ready to take cover when you try to throw it all the way to the plate."

Napoleon leaned in and looked at Wellington with a trace of a smile before he went slowly into his windup. With perfect form, he whipped the ball around and threw a perfect fastball. Before Groh could move, the ball caught the inside corner of the plate and struck the top of the thin bat handle just above his hands. It bounced off the bat in a weak imitation of a bunt. Groh started to run for first, but Arthur picked up the slow roller and threw easily to Abe at first. Groh was out by a mile. He was clearly humiliated. As he walked back to his dugout, Napoleon stepped toward him and said something. Groh turned and started to walk to the mound, but a sharp word from the manager McGraw brought him to heel. Groh turned and walked contritely back to the dugout.

Next up was Ty Cobb. As he approached the plate, there was an ominous howling from the right field stands. He said nothing to Napoleon, but glared with red eyes at the pitcher. The pitch came fast, but Cobb swung fiercely and connected. Napoleon ducked as a line drive went by his ear and landed clean in left center, barely clearing Danny's glove. Cobb rounded first and took a long lead before Wilde pegged a throw from left center to Danny, cutting off Cobb.

Cobb took a smaller lead from first, and Honus Wagner stepped to the plate. Compared to Groh and Cobb, he seemed genuinely happy to be playing. He took a few practice cuts and hit a grounder off the third pitch to short. Dickens picked it up easily and shoveled an underhanded throw to Danny at second. Danny turned and got the ball off to Abe for the second out, but wasn't ready for what happened next. He saw Cobb coming at him, completely horizontal and airborne with razor sharp cleats pointed directly at Danny's thigh. Danny had never seen anyone slide so high.

He had no time to think, but fortunately Yoshida Shoin had come in from center just behind Danny to back him up. While Cobb was still airborne, Yoshida was suddenly in front of Danny. He moved slightly and seemed to lightly brush the airborne Cobb. The little push was just enough to throw him off course, and he flew by Danny past second and into short center field. The crowd was quiet for a moment, then realized they had just seen a double play. They roared approval.

Tris Speaker, the left fielder, stepped up to bat in the cleanup spot. He was tall and rangy, with arms that looked like steel cables. He appeared to be completely focused on the game. Speaker appeared to look right through the pitcher and dispassionately take in the whole ballpark with a glance, not unlike a predator.

His relative calm appeared to unnerve Napoleon a little. He shook off two signs from Arthur, who walked out to the mound to calm his pitcher. When he returned to behind the plate, Napoleon threw a shaky curve which looked as if it would be a mile outside. Speaker stepped across the plate and swung with the most powerful motion Danny had ever seen. He hit the ball cleanly and it screamed off the bat as it headed down the third base line. The ball was traveling almost too fast to see, but Fredrick moved just as quickly. He jumped skyward no less than two feet off the ground with his glove fully extended and caught the ball on the fly. The stadium exploded with cheers.

The Dodgers ran off the field to the dugout, clapping Douglas on the back. As he ran from the field, he was surprised when Speaker ran over and patted his arm. "Hell of a catch, Mr. Douglass. Hell of a catch." He smiled. "Watch out for the next one, though. I'm going to put it in your ear."

Douglass looked at the country boy and replied in a polite, even tone. "Maybe I'll put one in yours."

Speaker paused thoughtfully. "Sounds like we got a deal." He caught his glove that Cobb had brought out from the dugout and ran out to left field.

Chapter 13

The leadoff hitter for the Dodgers was Fredrick Douglass, who walked up to the plate with complete confidence in spite of the fierce warmup pitches of the opposing team's starter, Smoky Joe Wood. Wood threw with a compact motion and short windup, and his pitches gave the impression of being shot from a rifle. Wood threw right-handed, and Douglass settled in to bat left-handed. He was a natural righty. Danny had noticed him hitting left-handed one day and asked him what he was doing. "Moving one step closer to first base", came the answer.

The first pitch was a hard fastball right down the middle, and he swung high and missed it. He took the second pitch for a ball, and then swung hard at an inside curveball. He hit it solid, and the ball went over the infield and took a short hop to right center. Douglas sped down the line to first. As he ran, he noticed that Frank Chance was not moving to make a play from the outfield. Instead of placing his foot on the bag and leaning toward the throw, he looked at Douglas and planted himself firmly in front of the bag. He was an imposingly big man, with legs like small tree trunks and a massively muscular upper body. However, Douglass was also strong and was very compact. When he saw Chance blocking the bag, he lowered his body, tucked his head, and lunged into the bigger man with no hesitation. When they collided, there was a *crack!* and Chance was knocked clean out of the basepath onto the infield grass. He held his right ankle and glared at Douglass, who was brushing himself off at first and stopped to smile broadly at Chance. It looked like Chance wanted to get up and charge Douglas, but his ankle was bent at a grotesque angle and he was unable to move from his position. Marshall, the home plate umpire, called time and a small squad of stretcher bearers removed Chance from the field. A new player came from the dugout.

As Chance was carried off, Douglas ignored him and took a healthy lead away from Stuffy McInnis, the new first baseman. Danny came to bat and felt the same butterflies in his stomach he'd noticed on the walk over to the stadium. This pitcher was fast. Faster than anyone he'd ever seen before. He was also accurate and seemed to throw only strikes. Almost before he settled in and took his stance, the ball rocketed past him. Startled, Danny stepped out of the box and backed away a step. He glanced at Douglas, who leaned forward as he led off from first. He gave Danny an unexpected wink and grin, just as Calamity called out from the dugout, "Let's go, Danny boy! Go yard!" When he saw Fredrick wink and heard Calamity call for him to hit a homer, something shifted in him and the butterflies disappeared. His whole body relaxed and suddenly he felt like a coiled spring, ready to play.

As he stepped back to the plate, he looked directly in Smoky Joe's eyes. What he saw, or didn't see, surprised him. There was a complete lack of interest and a vacant, hollow look. As he took his stance, Danny realized that this was just a job for the pitcher. There was a complete lack of excitement or joy on his face, and it was clear that he didn't really care whether Danny hit the ball or not. For some reason, Danny felt he'd found a weakness. He loved every single second of what was happening, and the man on the mound looked as if he'd be just as happy or unhappy doing anything else.

He looked over at the dugout and saw Babbage give the signal to steal.

Danny smiled at the pitcher, who seemed taken aback. This time, when he threw, Danny lunged forward and took a wild, wide swing at the ball. Using this interference; Douglas took off for second as if he'd been launched, and easily beat the throw. He dusted himself off and looked at Honus Wagner, who had wisely chosen not to block the basepath.

There was a man on second and nobody out. The attitude of the visiting team seemed to be shifting. They had thought they were in for a romp, and suddenly they found themselves in a ball game. Double plays, leaping catches, baserunning collisions, game ending injuries—all in the first inning. Smoky Joe Wood glanced over his shoulder nervously at second, then back at the plate. Again, Danny gave him a wide smile, enjoying the fact that it seemed to upset the pitcher. He tried to show every tooth in his mouth. Wood leaned back and fired the ball right at Danny.

Danny was ready. He leaned back and let the ball pass in front of him. The count was one ball and one strike. He knew the pitcher would try to throw a strike to avoid being behind in the count. He leaned into the plate. The ball came right down the middle, and Danny felt just like it had shot out of the same batting machines on which he'd spent hours and hours practicing. He took a perfect swing and hit the pitch square.

The ball hit the ground between third and short, then shot into the outfield for a base hit. Douglas went to third and Danny made it to first in front of the throw. However, when the first baseman caught the throw he still tagged Danny hard by swinging his glove and hitting him in the back. Danny reached back to rub his low spine and looked up at McInnis.

"Just letting you know, kid", the first baseman said, "That by the time this game is over you'll wish Chance was still in. I ain't no second stringer."

"I know who you are", said Danny. "You were part of the famous $100,000 infield with the Athletics in 1911."

McInnis obviously liked the recognition. "That's right, punk. And don't forget it."

This time it was Danny's turn to trash talk. "How could I forget? We laugh at it now. Even the rookies off the farm average twenty times that money now in the big leagues. They spend the amount of your salary on chewing tobacco."

The first baseman flushed. He moved next to Danny and stood face to face. Danny enjoyed the fact that he was actually taller than McInnis and didn't move.

"By the way", said Danny, "If you hit me in the back with another cheap shot like that, I'm going to pull the ball out of your glove and stuff it down your throat. Then they'll have a whole new reason to call you Stuffy." With this he pushed his face even closer to McInnis. The first base umpire stepped between them, and McInnis went back to his position.

Oscar Wilde was third in the batting order and swung the bat slowly as he left the on deck circle. He was 6'3" and looked even taller next to the relatively shorter men around him. On the team, only Lincoln stood taller. He appeared anything but nervous, and, more than anyone, he was clearly enjoying the crowd and competition. He waved to the crowd prior to stepping in the batter's box and took his stance. The stands responded with wild cheers, and he seemed to stand even taller feeling the love of the people. Wood stood back from the mound, watching both runners, completely bewildered at the tall man who appeared so comfortable in front of a stadium-sized audience.

Finally, he stepped to the mound and threw from a quick stretch. The crowd expected a big swing and were surprised when he expertly laid a bunt down the first base line. Both runners had a jump on the ball and ran before the bunt. Connie Mack came out from behind the plate and snagged the ball. It looked as if Fredrick and Danny had him beat, so he angrily threw out Oscar at first, clearly upset that both runners had each successfully made the next base standing up.

Oscar tipped his hat to the crowd and disappeared into the dugout, while Lincoln walked to the plate, fourth in the batting order. There was a reverential hush in the stadium, in stark contrast to the boisterous noise a minute before. He noticed the complete quiet and stopped short of the batter's box. He turned to the crowd and called time out.

"Folks", he said. "Out here, I'm not the rail-splitter from Springfield. I'm just one of the ballplayers. If I don't hear some noise, I'll start to feel like nobody likes me. So, carry on, please."

This charmed the crowd, and the stadium exploded with cheers. Abe grinned and stepped into the box. On the mound, Wood was visibly losing patience with the celebrity aspect of the Dodgers and started to bear down. On the second pitch, Lincoln hit a high fly into deep center. Danny stayed close to the bag, and for a moment thought the ball was out of the park. Cobb drifted back, then jumped up with his back to the fence and speared the ball. Douglas and Danny tagged up, and Fredrick scored easily. Danny held up at third and scored a moment later when Calamity singled. The inning ended with the Dodgers up 2-0 when Dickens grounded into a double play. As he walked out to second, Danny had his eyes out for a hot dog vendor, but all he could see in the stands was concession salesmen handing out a bread-like substance. Finally, he heard the cry he'd been waiting for. "Hot Dogs!" he heard from just behind the home dugout. Danny's grin grew and he promised himself to get at least one dog before the day was over.

The next few innings were just as intense. It was a game of skill versus enthusiasm. The visitors no longer seemed so confident; on the other hand, as the innings went by, the home team grew surer of themselves and seemed to be having more fun. They were chanting, cheering, and playing fearless ball. There were moments that brought the crowd to their feet, and occasionally rocked the stadium with laughter. In the top of the 4th inning, Wahoo Sam Crawford led off the inning with a single to right. Jane caught the ball on the first bounce and threw hurriedly to first. Abe caught the ball too late to tag out Crawford. Keeping an eye on Crawford, he walked out to the mound and said a few calming words to Napoleon. With the ball still in his glove, he jogged back over to first and took his stance.

Crawford looked a Lincoln, and after some hesitation spoke humbly as he started to lead off.

"Mr. President. It's an honor to share the field with you."

Lincoln glanced sideways at him, and said, "You have me at a disadvantage, sir, since you know me and I am not acquainted with you."

"I'm Sam Crawford from Wahoo, Nebraska. I'm a ballplayer but do know my history."

Napoleon was still not set on the mound, so Lincoln turned and extended his hand.

"It's a pleasure to meet you."

Crawford moved toward Lincoln, just off the base, and extended his hand. As he did, Lincoln looked at the first base umpire, who was watching them intently. With a sly smile, Lincoln shook hands with Crawford, touched his opponent with his glove, then nonchalantly took the ball out and tossed it over to a waiting Napoleon.

"You're out!" The umpire shouted to Wahoo Sam.

Crawford was shocked. He stood dumbfounded for a moment. As he turned to walk away he spoke angrily to Lincoln. "They called you Honest Abe! I can't believe you'd use the hidden ball trick."

Lincoln smiled. "Don't forget, I was a lawyer a lot longer than I was President. There's nothing dishonest about taking advantage of someone who's not paying attention. It was still nice to meet you, Sam."

Crawford stalked back to the dugout, embarrassed but wiser. The ball went around the horn and back to Napoleon. He took the ball and looked at the plate. Napoleon Lajoie stood in the box, at bat. The pitcher nodded to him.

"Bonjour", said Napoleon. "I appreciate your parents' respect for our history." Then he threw a strike, barely catching the inside corner of the plate.

Lajoie stepped out of the batter's box. He looked at John Marshall. "Can't you shut him up?"

Marshall looked at him with contempt. "Can't you? Are you afraid?"

Lajoie sneered and said as he stepped back in the box, "Quit yammering. I don't know who I'm named after."

Napoleon stepped on the rubber and just before winding up said, *"Oui.* I'm not surprised you know little of our country's history. Looking at you, I see the kind of man who would have cowered in a barn while we marched to victory." Then he threw another strike, this time barely catching the outside of the plate. Lajoie grew red and stepped out of the box again. He was shaking with anger. On the mound, Buonaparte took his time. He spoke again.

"I'm going to strike you out, *mon ami*. There is nothing you can do about it. No matter where or when we meet, I will always triumph. I will triumph because I was born to rule, and you were born to follow." Lajoie's face tensed with rage. There was a windup, and Napoleon appeared to be ready to deliver a fastball. At the last second, his delivery slowed and he threw a completely unexpected, softly floating changeup.

Lajoie almost fell in front of the plate swinging at the ball. He was clearly off balance and missed by a more than a foot. He threw the bat down and started to charge the mound.

Marshall, from behind home plate, said calmly, "Stop."

Lajoie turned. "Or what?", he said in a mildly threatening way.

Marshall picked up on his defiant tone immediately and seemed to relish the challenge.

"Or I'll throw you right out of the game."

Lajoie became even angrier. Before he could stop himself, a thin stream of tobacco flew in a perfect arc from his mouth and landed in the dirt at Marshall's feet. Marshall looked down and noticed a small drop had bounced onto his left shoe. He looked at Lajoie and gestured with his right thumb. "You're gone!" He shouted.

Lajoie paused but quickly realized the futility of his situation. The crowd was beginning to boo—something he clearly wasn't used to. He headed to his dugout with the General's taunt following him: "*Au revoir, mon ami. Back to the barn.*"

The other Napoleon walked silently back to the dugout and was gone a moment later. As he did, a shout came from the outfield and the second base umpire called time and ran to home plate. Marshall stopped out to meet him.

"What can I help you with, Ump?"

The second base umpire cleared his throat. "I'm not sure you can throw that man out for some tobacco juice on your shoe."

Marshall took off his face mask and stepped closer to the second base umpire. "What's your name, son?"

The second base umpire shifted a bit. "Holmes. Oliver Wendell Holmes."

The home plate umpire looked at him quizzically. "Did you read the manual, Mr. Holmes?"

Holmes looked at the dirt. "No," he confessed.

Marshall placed his hand on Holmes' shoulder. "I'm a little offended. I wrote that book. Do you know how to read?"

The second base ump appeared to be getting upset. "Of course, I can read. I was a Supreme Court Justice."

Marshall appeared unimpressed. "Then you know who I am. And if you'd read that book, you'd know I can throw you out just as fast as I threw him out. Now get back out there behind second base and don't ask any more questions you already know the answer to."

Just then the very heavy man umpiring third base walked up to the two of them and raised his hand. He started to speak, but before he could get a word out Marshall cut him off without even looking at him.

"Don't even think about arguing with me, Taft. Get lost." The heavy man turned and walked defeatedly away. A lone cheer echoed from the right first base line, right where Roosevelt was sitting.

Following this, Holmes obeyed and went back to behind second base, and the game resumed.

Connie Mack was next up. He was a thin, tall man who played like he was the smartest one on the team. He stepped politely into the box, and on the first pitch hit a fast grounder heading into the gap between first and second base. Danny dove to his left and caught the ball on the second bounce, then shoveled the ball to Abe just before Mack's foot hit the bag.

Danny got up and trotted back to the dugout, looking at the scoreboard. It was still 2-0.

Chapter 14

The teams played even ball until the top of the sixth inning. At that point the strong skills of the visiting team began to wear on Napoleon as he faced the top of the batting order. He managed to get Groh to fly out. Cobb hissed and wheezed trying to run out a ground ball as Dickens threw him out. However, when Honus Wagner came up, Napoleon began to tire. Wagner hit the second pitch for a double off the left field wall. Speaker came up next and, on a 2-2 count, hit over the center field fence for a home run. As he passed third while trotting around the bases, he passed Douglass and smiled broadly. "We'll see who smiling when it's over, my friend," Douglass said.

Charlie Babbage came out to the mound. Napoleon appeared reluctant to leave, but after a moment handed the ball to Babbage. As he walked off the field, the crowd stood and applauded. He flushed with pleasure and for a moment appeared to again be the man that could conquer the world.

The bullpen gate swung open, and Simon Bolivar jogged to the mound. As he approached the mound, a large contingent of men and women behind the home dugout stood and began to sing a powerful anthem. Wellington and Danny met him at the mound. "What are they singing?", asked Danny.

Bolivar paused reflectively as he took the ball from Arthur. "A song I haven't heard for many, many years. It's *La Marcha Libertadora*. It was the anthem of our revolution." He looked over at the standing, singing crowd. He listened reverently for a moment. Then he looked at Wellington. "Those are my people. We are going to win this game."

Arthur nodded. "*Si, General,*" he said with no trace of a British accent. He patted Simon on the arm with his glove and jogged back to the plate.

Bolivar had a completely different manner on the mound than Napoleon, who had displayed an icy cool. Bolivar was just the opposite. He paced the mound like a caged tiger until the batter came up. He then stepped to the center of the mound, bent forward with the ball in his glove, and stared. He dangled his right arm loosely at his side, rhythmically shaking his hand to a beat only he could hear. Stuffy McInnis was in the batter's box, clearly ruffled by what he was seeing on the mound.

"Throw the ball!" He shouted. Bolivar kept staring at him, shaking his right hand and moving the fingers. McInnis appeared to be about to shout again, but before any words could come out Simon straightened up, took the ball, and with almost no windup fired a ball so fast that those sitting near the field could hear it hum. McInnis had no time to even get the bat off his shoulder.

"Strike!", yelled Marshall.

Danny jumped up. "Way to hum, Simon. Chuck it, buddy!"

The rest of the dugout joined in. Yoshida called out, "Can't hit, can't hit, can't hit!" Soon the entire dugout was chanting and shouting. The other dugout remained sullen and dead silent, as if they wouldn't dream of cheering for anyone other than themselves.

Encouraged by the noise, Bolivar felt strengthened. After two more quick pitches, consisting of a swerving curveball and another humming fastball, McInnis sat back down in his dugout, cursing under his breath. The next two batters went down just as easy, and the inning was over.

Looking out of the dugout, Danny expected to see Smoky Joe Wood walking to the mound. Instead, there was a tall young left hander walking very deliberately onto the field from the bullpen. Danny didn't recognize him and looked quizzically at Babbage.

Charlie looked at his papers and looked back at Danny. "That's George Ruth. This boy is quite a pitcher. In one season he had nine shutouts, and at one point he pitched 29 scoreless World Series innings. We're going to have our hands full."

"Wow." Danny said. "Babe Ruth the pitcher. It's like seeing young Elvis. Except he can throw a baseball very well."

Danny looked at the infield to see who was replacing Lajoie. Now at second, there was a tall African American man who moved with easy grace around the infield, and snapped his throws like bullets. He glanced briefly at the home team dugout, then turned his attention back to the field.

"Who's playing second?" Danny asked Babbage.

Babbage checked his papers. "That's Mr. John Henry Lloyd. His nickname was 'Pops'. He played in the segregated leagues. Their pitcher, George Ruth, said Mr. Lloyd was the greatest player who ever lived. So, they're certainly not short on talent."

The first batter to face Ruth was Yoshida. He tried to read the pitcher, to get a feeling for what to expect. Instead, he found a face of stone and complete concentration. There was a brief windup and a hard pitch which, while not as fast as Wood's, seemed even more difficult to hit.

There was a ball, then another strike, and then Shoin got his bat on the ball. He hit it hard, and it flew over the shortstop's head into left field. It looked like a sure base hit, but Tris Speaker sprinted to the ball and made a diving catch.

Cathay Williams came in for Charles Dickens at shortstop and was now batting seventh. She stared right back at Ruth, and hit a line drive off his first pitch. She made it to first easily. However, the next two batters were easily retired and the inning ended. Ruth walked slowly off the mound, looking stronger now than when he started.

Bolivar came back out to the mound as he seventh inning started. The first batter was the new second baseman, John Henry Lloyd. He stepped to the plate, his face impassive. Bolivar tried to intimidate him but received only a friendly nod and smile in return. His first pitch was high and outside for a ball. His second pitch was a curveball, but as it crossed the plate Lloyd stepped forward with a deceptively effortless swing and hit the ball square. The hit was a high arching fly ball which dropped like a shot between Shoin and Wilde. Oscar grabbed the ball and threw to second, where Danny caught it just a moment slower than needed to tag Lloyd out. It was a standup double, and Bolivar was clearly shaken at how easy that had been for John Henry.

The visitor's pitcher walked slowly to the plate. He was tall and appeared strong. His muscles rippled under his jersey. Cathay was playing short now, and she tried to shout some encouragement. "It's the pitcher, Simon. He won't be able to hit. Easy out here!"

Danny saw the expression on Ruth's face change from flat to angry when he heard Cathay refer to him as an easy out. He shifted his feet and planted them firmly in the box. He then reached out and pointed his bat to the center field fence. Most of the players were confused by this, but Danny started to worry as Ruth held the bat steady and looked slowly around the field. Danny glanced in the dugout and saw Babbage shake his head ruefully. Bolivar wound up and threw a hard fastball slightly inside. Danny's jaw dropped as Ruth whipped the bat around to hit. It was a combination of speed and power like Danny had never seen before. Nobody in this game so far—not Cobb, not Speaker, not anybody—had swung the bat like that. There was an audible crack that could be heard throughout the whole stadium, and the ball screamed directly into center field, with Bolivar, then Danny, then Wilde watching helplessly as it left the stadium, still rising as it went out of sight.

Ruth stood for a second, his body twisted, both hands gripping the bat in a perfect follow through, and watched the ball leave the field. There was no smile, but Danny thought he saw a look of satisfaction cross his face as he gently set down the bat and trotted casually around the bases. It was now 4-2 against the Dodgers. Danny jogged to the mound. He was glad to see that Bolivar seemed steady.

"You're doing fine, Simon. You might have just faced the two greatest players ever, and even they won't hit it every time. We'll get them next time."

Bolivar nodded in response and smiled. "Thank you, my young *amigo*. I can sometimes recall facing down the royal artillery at Boyacá. As you say, I'll get the next ones and at least am in no danger of losing my arms or legs." After speaking, he returned to his hawk-like pitching position as Danny returned to second base.

Heinie Groh was up. Simon wound up and threw another curve which spun toward the inside corner. Groh tried to lift the pitch and instead topped it, and the ball rolled slowly to the mound. Bolivar picked it up and threw without looking directly into Abe's glove at first base. He was out. Groh stopped halfway down the first base line and spat into the dirt on his way back to the dugout.

Cobb came up next. He leaned in aggressively and glared with anger at Bolivar. For this, he was brushed back by a high inside fastball at the shoulders. This seemed to enrage him further, and he cursed as he stepped back into the box, but Danny noticed he didn't crowd the plate as much after that.

The next pitch was low and outside, and Cobb lunged angrily to hit it. It struck the outside of the bat and flew foul into the right field stands. Calamity Jane ran over to try to catch the ball on the fly but stopped well short when the ball headed into the far right stands. She saw Applegate again in the midst of all the dark, shapeless forms, looking directly at her. While staring into her eyes, he held up his left hand and without looking caught the ball on the fly. With his right hand, he smiled and again beckoned her with his right index finger. It was well known to all that she feared nothing in this life or any other, but now she appeared to want to be anywhere else but around him. She backed slowly away. When he saw her take a step back, he immediately lost interest, looked elsewhere, and flipped the ball over his shoulder. A great wailing from the crowd ensued, and the same ring of flames opened to swallow the ball.

The rest of the crowd continued to cheer. Apparently the writhing, unfortunate mass of souls was nothing unexpected or unusual to anyone else. Bolivar again focused on Cobb. He leaned in and shook his right hand rhythmically until he could see Cobb staring at the wiggling hand. He quickly moved his hand to his glove and with a rapid motion threw the pitch. It was clear that Cobb wasn't quite set, and he tried to check his initial swing but couldn't. A small pop fly over shortstop resulted, and Cathay caught it while staring at Cobb and barely looking at the ball. Cobb stood watching incredulously, and when she caught it, he shouted, "I have over 4,000 hits!" Cathay smiled and flipped the ball underhanded to Bolivar.

"Not against us, angry man. Not against us." She turned her back to him and walked back to short. John Marshall stepped out in front of the plate and tapped Cobb on the shoulder.

"Back to the dugout or out of the park, pepper pot."

Cobb whirled around at the tap and saw that it had been Marshall. Suddenly subdued, he walked over and carefully replaced his bat. As he stepped toward the dugout, Honus Wagner walked past him and stood in the batter's box.

Wagner took a natural, balanced stance and waited for the pitch. The infield shifted slightly to the left. Bolivar took a long, slow windup and fired a fastball which smacked the glove of the catcher in a blink. Two more pitches were curveballs just outside of the strike zone, and then one dropped in for a 2-3 count. A final fastball just off the wrists struck him out to end the top of the seventh inning.

The organist started to play, and the entire audience except for the far right field grandstand stood for the seventh inning stretch. It seemed like at least a hundred different languages combined to create quite possibly the most unusual rendition of "Take Me Out to the Ball Game" ever sung, while both teams regrouped to plan their next moves. With the scoreboard showing a 4-2 visitor's lead, the Dodgers came up in the bottom of the seventh.

Douglass was up to bat. He fouled the first two pitches, and then correctly anticipated a change up from Ruth and hit a blooper to right center. It looked like a typical single, but he broke into a sprint after reaching first. The throw from Cobb to second went over the second baseman's head and was stopped by the catcher, who fired back to second. He slid safely under the tag of John Henry Lloyd and got up to brush himself off.

John Henry tossed the ball back to Ruth and took his stance in the infield. As Douglass started to take a lead off second, Lloyd spoke in a low voice.

"Reverend Douglass. I'm John Henry Lloyd." Douglas turned and nodded to the second baseman, still wary of a pickoff attempt.

Lloyd continued. "Thank you for teaching that first baseman a lesson. He had it coming and you gave it to him."

Douglas nodded again, and said, "He was blocking the baseline. That's not healthy, and that's all I was trying to teach him. I didn't mean to hurt him.

This time John Henry nodded. "That being said, sir," he continued and then paused briefly, "If I'm on the basepath and you run into me, you'd best try hitting a brick wall first so you'll have an idea of what it will feel like."

Douglas showed a slight smile. "I have no doubt you're sturdy, Mr. Lloyd. However, I have extensive experience running into brick walls, so I certainly know what to expect. And I've knocked down more than a few."

As Lloyd turned his attention back to Ruth and saw Danny settle into the box, he replied, "That you have, sir. That you have."

At bat, Danny couldn't help feeling nervous. He was facing the man who many regarded as the greatest baseball player who ever lived.

As he took the first pitch, he realized that Ruth may have been an even greater pitcher than he was a hitter. He had almost perfect control and threw with uncanny accuracy. He varied his pitch speed as much as he varied his placement. Danny fouled the first pitch down the third base line, then swung at two more to strike out. He walked dejectedly back to the dugout and sat down. The Mayor appeared at his side, took out a small paper bag and handed to him. The bag felt warm. It was printed with distinctive, old fashioned font spelling out **EBBETS FIELD CONCESSIONS**.

Jacob saw his puzzled look, and said, "You said you wanted a hot dog at Ebbets field."

Danny looked in the bag. There was indeed a good-sized hot dog in the bag, just the way he liked it—ketchup only. He looked back at Jacob. "I can't eat it now. I'm in the middle of the game."

Jacob looked at him quietly for a moment. "It's almost time. Things are finally getting in order. I don't know if you'll be able to finish the game."

Danny felt his stomach knot. "Please. Just two more innings. I want to help win. So far I haven't done anything."

Jacob again placed a comforting hand on his shoulder. "Bigger forces than I can control have been set in motion. To be honest, I don't want you to go anywhere. But the universe is correcting itself the only way it can."

Danny stared sadly at the hot dog and set the bag down on the bench next to him. "Okay," and turned his gaze back to the game. Oscar was up, and ahead in the count 3-1 It looked a bit like Ruth might be tiring. On the next pitch, he hit a hard grounder which was barely stopped by John Henry Lloyd. The second baseman looked at Douglas, faked a throw to third, then threw to first. The fake didn't fool Douglas, who slid hard into third under the throw from McInnis.

It was two out. Charlie Babbage put down his clipboard and stood on the dugout steps, leaning on the rail. He looked at Abe walking up to bat, then at Fredrick carefully leading off third. He touched the brim of his hat casually.

Abe crowded the plate, leaning far inside. It was almost an invitation to get hit by the next pitch. Ruth backed up a little, hesitated, then started his windup more slowly than usual. He didn't expect Fredrick Douglas to sprint down the line to home, and as he saw the man barreling toward the plate his control was shaken. He threw high and outside, and although Connie Mack lunged and grabbed the ball as fast as he could, he couldn't reach the far corner of the plate as Douglas slid in headfirst and touched the base. Now it was 4-3.

When the commotion at the plate died down, Lincoln stepped back into the batter's box.

Ruth appeared a bit shaken by the steal and stepped away from the mound for a moment. When he composed himself, he stepped back to the rubber and wound up. He threw a fastball, and Abe caught it square for a double off the right field wall. Sam Crawford got the ball to second just in time to stop Lincoln from taking third. Unfortunately for the home team, Calamity hit a high fly ball to left field and Jackson caught it with no difficulty. The inning was over.

In the top of the eighth, Simon continued to pitch like a master. He retired Speaker, McInnis, and Mack consecutively with various pop flies and grounders. The visiting team went down grumbling and making excuses for their play, which didn't seem to earn the sympathy of John

McGraw as he shouted at each one as they entered the dugout.

The bottom of the eighth inning didn't go much better for the Dodgers. Yoshida Shoin started off strong with a single to center field, and Cathay Williams followed with a short hop single to shallow left field that moved Yoshida to second base. However, when Wellington came up, he hit a hard grounder directly to Wagner, who then made the play of the game. All at once, he tagged Shoin, touched the base to get Cathay out, and then threw a bullet to first which barely beat Wellington. It was a triple play, and the crowd jumped to their feet in amazement and cheered. As always, Wagner was modest but did unexpectedly stop to tip his hat on the way into the dugout. The crowd loved it, and Cobb glared at him as he passed to the dugout. Wagner just smiled.

It was the top of the ninth. Bolivar strode confidently to the mound. He looked strong, and as he warmed up, he seemed to be throwing with more accuracy and speed than ever. Wahoo Sam Crawford came up to bat and tipped the third pitch to hit a shallow fly to right field, which Calamity caught near the foul line. She ignored the howling from the grandstand and threw the ball back to Bolivar.

John Henry Lloyd walked to the plate and set himself with determination. The first pitch was fast—so fast that he barely got the bat off his shoulder and started to swing before it hit the catcher' mitt. He stepped back for a moment, impressed. He nodded at Bolivar, then said, "Let's try that again." He stepped back into the box. This time a curve which broke wildly from inside to out caught him looking as it was called a strike. Finally, Bolivar threw a slow, off-speed pitch which Lloyd hit for an awkward pop fly, easily caught by Danny at second. As he threw the ball back to Bolivar, he thought he heard a strange, beeping echo for a moment. He trotted up to the mound.

"Did you hear that?", he asked Simon.

Bolivar looked at him curiously. "I heard nothing, *amigo*. Maybe the stadium has echoes that you hear better."

Reassured, he returned to his position. The trim George Herman Ruth walked grimly from the on-deck circle and took his place in front of the catcher, ready to hit. The stadium was quiet, and there was no chatter from Danny's team. Even Bolivar seemed to lose a little of his self-assurance facing the man who would become the Babe. The outfield moved back, close to the walls.

The pitcher took his time and wound up carefully. As the pitch came, Danny heard him grunt with effort as he threw as hard as he could. It was a great pitch—an inside fastball which hummed to the plate. However, Ruth swung perfectly. There was a loud *crack!* as he connected. Danny's heart sank with the sound of what was surely going to be a home run. The ball rocketed over second base, rising into center field. Oscar Wilde ran back to the fence as the ball started to arc down, looking as if it would clear the fence by a few feet. Wilde crouched then jumped. He strained to use every inch of his frame and reached over the top of the fence to catch the ball on the fly.

Oscar lost his balance as he made the catch and fell to the ground in a heap. He jumped up immediately, though, and proudly held up the ball. It was an incredible catch. Even Ruth, who had justifiably assumed it was a home run and began a leisurely trot around the bases, stopped to watch. When he saw Wilde make the catch, he stopped running, gave a brief salute to the center fielder, and turned to the dugout.

The Dodgers left the field for the bottom of the ninth, still down by a run. On the way in, Oscar jogged next to Danny. Unable to help himself, he asked Danny. "Did I just get a salute from the greatest player of all time?"

Danny had to grin. "You did, Oscar. And you deserved it. What a great play." Oscar beamed and took the steps down into the dugout, where he received several varied interpretations of the high five Danny had attempted to teach them.

As the inning started, Ruth was nowhere to be seen coming to the mound. For a few minutes, it was empty. Danny peered over into the visitor's dugout, and saw McGraw approach a man sitting far from the others at the end of the bench. The bullpen was empty, so he assumed McGraw was sending a pitcher from the dugout. They appeared to argue for a moment, and then the man got up and came out of the field. He was unshaven and looked angry. He gave a poisonous look toward the Dodgers and took the mound.

Charlie Babbage stood by Danny. "I was hoping they wouldn't use this fellow. He throws pitches we haven't seen before."

"How could that be?", asked Danny. "We've seen every pitch anybody throws."

Babbage shook his head ruefully. "This is Burleigh Grimes. He was the last player allowed to throw a spitball, and according to all reports, it was almost impossible to hit."

A look of recognition came over Danny's face. "Oh, this guy. I know about him. He used to chew tree bark and spit it on the ball. He'd use tobacco as well. He also was not a happy person. He actually threw a pitch at a player in the on-deck circle once."

Fredrick Douglass heard them discussing the pitcher and came over to listen. Danny explained brought him up to speed. "I remember learning that his spitballs break away from the right side of the plate to the left. He will also throw right at you, so be careful."

Fredrick nodded, and stepped out of the dugout for a few practice swings while Grimes warmed up. Every few pitches, he looked at the Dodgers as if he wanted to speak. Finally, he turned to the dugout.

"You ain't the real Dodgers, and you weren't even Brooklyn's team. I played for the real team, the Brooklyn Robins. We were better and classier than you bunch could ever be, and Ebbets field was built for us. I'm going to set you down like a bad piece of meat. You ain't winning this ball game."

Danny raised an eyebrow and looked at Babbage. "I hate to admit it, but he's got a point. The Dodgers were the Robins from 1914 to 1931. The uniforms didn't say "Dodgers" until 1932."

Babbage wrinkled his brow. "I still can't quite understand why that would make him so disagreeable."

"I suspect that he's the kind of guy who may be looking for reasons to get angry," replied Danny. He turned and selected a bat, then started up the dugout steps to the on-deck circle as Fredrick went to bat. As he walked up the stairs, he heard the same brief echo of an intermittent beeping or chime of some sort, which stopped almost as soon as it started. He shrugged it off and took a few swings as he watched Douglass at bat.

Grimes stood for a second on the mound, then while staring at Douglass reached in his pocket and pulled out a messy clump of brown fiber.

Danny sighed. *Elm bark*, he thought. *His favorite ball treatment.*

The angry-looking pitcher took his time, licked his fingers, and rubbed the dark wet clump around one side of the ball. The crowd responded with a disgusted moan. Grimes looked up and around the crowd, doing his best to communicate that he didn't care whether or not they approved of his pitching style.

He threw the ball, which hooked crazily on the way to the plate. Having been forewarned, Douglass gave it time to spin to the outside and then swung. As he hit the ball, brown liquid flew off and there was the sound of hitting a bag of dripping laundry. The ball went foul down the right base line and into the shapeless forms in the stands. This time, however, instead of the ball disappearing, it was immediately thrown back on to the field.

Seeing this, Danny had to smile. *Cubs fans*, he said to himself. *That's where they go.*

A decidedly unenthusiastic Sam Crawford picked up the ball between his thumb and forefinger, then with a grimace threw it back to the mound. Grimes caught it and smirked at Crawford. Then he turned to face Douglass. He again took out the bark, put a small amount in his mouth, then spit a large glob into his hand and rubbed it slowly on the ball. After a short windup, he threw again.

This time, when Grimes threw the wet ball, he leaned forward and laid a perfect bunt down the third base line. The spit-soaked ball didn't roll well, and stopped at an equal distance from home plate, third base, and the pitcher's mound. All three men ran to the ball and stopped for a split second to decide who would field it. This gave Douglass all the time needed to make it safely to first. Seeing this, Grimes angrily cursed Groh and Mack, who pointedly ignored him and walked back to their positions.

Danny walked to the plate, thinking about the score and how they needed two runs to win.

He was trying to focus, but he kept hearing the intermittent, irritating beeping noises. At bat, he decided to swing as hard as he could, given the spit ball's extra weight. Scowling as he threw, Grimes pitched the ball right at Danny who fell back into the dirt to avoid getting hit. The crowd booed, with the exception of the right field grandstand, who seemed to be cheering, making what sounded to Danny like a loud, strangling sound. He got up, dusted himself off, and stood back at the plate. He was angry at the brushback pitch.

As he stood at the plate, he shouted at Grimes. "Throw at me all you want. If you don't, I'm going to hit it." He paused. "By the way," he went on, "Nobody remembers you. Next to Newcombe, Koufax, Drysdale, Hershiser and Kershaw, you're a nobody who couldn't pitch without spitting on the ball. Do your worst."

As soon as he said it, he knew he'd let his anger get the best of him and he felt bad. For a minute after he finished speaking, Grimes looked hurt. Almost immediately, though, he snarled and started his wind up. The pitch looked inside, but Danny was ready and caught the outside curve of the pitch on the fat part of the bat.

The ball made another noise like a wet sack when it was hit, but took off with surprising velocity into right field. Danny felt like he'd never hit a ball so hard. He took off to first, and saw the ball strike the right field wall just inside the foul line and roll near the fence in front of the right field stands where Applegate stood just behind the wall, close to the field.

Danny ran at a full sprint around first and headed to second at breakneck speed. He could hear the Dodger dugout screaming for him and the crowd cheering with excitement. He rounded second and glanced toward right field. Crawford stood almost immobile in front of the grandstand, hesitating and hypnotized by the strange noises and shrieks coming from the monstrous forms in the seats. Applegate leered and beckoned to him. As he stood paralyzed with fear, Cobb sprinted his way at full speed to get the ball. Danny kept running.

As he approached third, he caught a glimpse of Christina, standing in the midst of a large group of people also on their feet. She stood out like she was being hit directly by a shaft of sunlight. Everyone around her was shouting and clapping, but she stood quietly, with a smile that struck him as both happy and sad. Impossibly, their eyes met. It looked as if she were trying to speak to him.

By this time, Cobb had shoved the immobilized Crawford out of the way and pivoted to throw. Danny rounded third and headed for the plate. Halfway there, he saw the ball coming and knew he'd have to slide into home. As he started his slide, time seemed to slow and the beeping, chiming echo came back, louder than ever. He let his momentum carry him into home plate, and at top speed, turned his body with his foot extended. Just as his foot touched the plate and John Marshall started to signal *safe!* he saw the ball miss Connie Mack's catcher's mitt. He tried to duck, but he felt he wasn't in control anymore. The ball slammed into his left temple. He was falling and traveling again, like he did so long ago before he woke up in the meadow. This time, though, instead of the silent dark blue which called him, he now heard noises and saw light. Unbearably bright light, with an ear-splitting accompaniment of beeping, chiming, and voices.

Chapter 15

Someone was pulling on his right eyelid and swinging a bright light back and forth close to his face. They weren't very gentle, and the light was painful. He raised a hand to push it away, but felt like he could barely move his arm. Finally, he managed to move the hand with the light away, and spoke. "Stop."

When he'd said this, he heard a woman's voice say his name, and then heard her voice break into sobbing. In the background the beeping and chiming continued all around him. With some effort, he opened both eyes and looked around. He was in bed, and on his right stood a doctor in a white coat covering surgical scrubs. He was tall and fit, with an air of quiet confidence. He looked past the doctor and saw the sobbing was coming from his mother. Tears streamed down her face, and she came forward and kissed his cheek. She looked worn, and her cheeks were hollow and thin. His father stood next to the doctor, visibly choked up with red eyes. He walked to the left side of the bed and kissed Danny as well. The doctor stepped forward and pressed a red button on a box behind the bed, and the beeping stopped.

"Monitor alarms", he explained. The doctor took his hand. "I'm Dr. Gerald Grant", he said. "I'm the neurosurgeon who operated on your head. We've been waiting for you to wake up for a long time." He squeezed Danny's hand. "Welcome back."

Danny looked around the room. "What day is it?" He asked. "Where am I?".

"It's September 23rd," replied Dr. Grant. "You're at Stanford University Medical Center. You've been unable to wake up for five months."

"Wow," said Danny. "It's Tommy Lasorda's birthday."

His Dad walked to him and put his hand on his left shoulder. "He's back, all right. He lives in the Dodger Universe."

"Why am I here?"

His Dad leaned closer to him. "You were hit in the head in the league championship game in April. You weren't doing well so we moved you from Phoenix to Stanford, and Dr. Grant found out you were accumulating fluid around your brain. He did surgery to relieve the pressure, and since then, we've been here with you. He told us he couldn't figure out why you weren't waking up, but not to give up hope. And now you're back."

Danny tried to move, but as he lifted his head everything spun, and his arms and legs felt like wood. He looked at his arm- it was skeleton thin. He felt his abdomen, where a small soft tube came out from the skin. His belly stung a little when he touched it.

"That's your feeding tube," his Mom said. "Don't pull on it. You were breathing fine after a while but couldn't swallow safely."

"We'll get it out soon," said Dr. Grant. "We just need to make sure you're swallowing okay. I don't think it will be a problem." He continued thoughtfully. "It's very unusual to see someone wake up and be as alert so suddenly. It makes me happy. I have a feeling you're going to make a complete recovery, but you're going to need a lot of rehab therapy."

Dr. Grant was right. The next several days blended together and mainly consisted of nonstop visits by physical therapists teaching him to walk, occupational therapists teaching him to take care of himself, and speech therapists working to fine tune his speech and thinking skills. After a month of rehab at Stanford, he went home to Arizona. After another month he was still stiff and easily tired, but after Thanksgiving, he was strong enough to start school again. He received a hero's welcome on his first day, and he'd forgotten how many friends he had. Somewhat surprisingly, he found himself thinking less and less often about the dream he must have had while unconscious. Although he couldn't explain why, he never felt comfortable discussing it with anyone. His time at the field remained his secret.

There is no better place to train than Arizona in winter. The day before Christmas Danny finally successfully talked his Dad into taking him to the batting cages after many previous attempts. He stepped into the large, netted alley facing the machine and held a bat for the first time since April. Pitch after pitch flew by him, while his timing and swing mechanics were too rusty to hit the ball. He looked at his Dad, who clearly thought it was too soon to be there. Finally, they were both tired.

"Just try to get your bat in front of it, son." He sounded as if he thought it was impossible.

"One more pitch," Danny said.

The machine whirred and a pitch shot out. Danny struggled to watch the ball into his bat. He swung with perfect timing and hit it dead center. The ball jumped off the bat and slammed into the netting at the end of the alley. His father's eyes widened, and jaw dropped as he put both hands in the air and shouted, "That's what I'm talking about!"

The drive home was much different than the trip out to the batting cages. His Dad talked excitedly about more training and hiring a personal coach to help. It was music to Danny's ears. Nothing about his injury bothered him more than not being able to play, and it looked like he was finally getting back on the field.

January, February, and March went by slowly as he worked. His parents had always thought he was dedicated to becoming a great baseball player, but what they saw over those months filled them with awe. School was from 8 to 3 every day, but he was up at 6 every morning. Those two hours were spent conditioning with weights, getting his flexibility back, and first walking and then running to build up speed and strength. After school, he'd have three hours of concentrated baseball with a coach his parents hired. They reviewed every aspect of the game from baserunning to hitting to fielding, and Danny felt his confidence grow.

Tryouts for the team eventually came, and he made the cut to play for his school as a sophomore. By the end of the season, he was starting at second on the varsity squad. His mother and father thought they were watching a different young man. He had always been cool under pressure, but now he played as if nothing frightened him. No matter who he faced, no matter what the situation, he seemed to think in a crystal clear fashion and respond perfectly. As he played, words seemed to come to him that would calm and reassure him. Underneath it all, he never lost the feeling that this was a game that should be fun. And most of all, he was having fun.

Time seemed to pass all out of sequence. After the initial few months crawled by, everything seemed to speed past. His high school years flew by, and his team won the Arizona state championship his senior year. He always considered himself a team player and shunned the spotlight. He was recruited to play on a full scholarship at ASU, and made the adjustment to college ball easily. During these years he was intensely focused on two things: baseball and his studies. Inspired by Dr. Grant to train in neurosurgery, he majored in biology and kept his grades near the top of his class.

People who knew Danny well worried about him overworking. He never dated or attended social events, and spent every minute either in the lab, library, or on the field. His friends and roommates just shook their head and called him "The Machine". In his senior and junior year, he was named to the all-league team at second base and led the team in batting.

Beginning in his junior year, he began to feel the pull of his studies more than he felt the need to be on the field. He'd had visits from pro baseball clubs about joining a team's farm system—even his beloved Dodgers sent a scout to visit. While Danny felt a twinge of regret, he somehow grew more confident that his future lay elsewhere, and the memories of his neurosurgeon kept coming back to him, making a greater impression as each year went by.

Eventually, he took his parents to dinner at their favorite restaurant in Phoenix and surprised them by explaining that he wanted to go to medical school instead of trying to play pro ball. When they asked why he didn't want to try to play ball before medical school, he revealed that he was considering neurosurgery. This would require four more years of medical school and seven of residency training. He went on to say that given the length of time needed for this training, even a few years away from school might put him far behind in his goals. When his Dad brought up money and stardom as motivation to play, he had to smile.

"It's never been about that, Dad. I play ball because it's fun, and I never want it to become a job." When he finished that sentence, he suddenly saw the hollow, disinterested stare of Smoky Joe Wood as he stood on the mound. He hadn't thought of that stare since waking up years ago. There had been hardly any recollections of what he had experienced and by now simply remembered it as a dream during the time he was out of commission, and the image of Smoky Joe sent a chill through his body. He wanted more than anything never to feel about baseball the way those eyes looked, and knew he was making the right decision. After this brief flashback, somehow it seemed easier to explain to his parents.

In his junior year, he tested to get into medical school and did very well. He applied to many schools, but when the offers for admission came there was only one school he was interested in.

"Georgetown?", his mother asked. Why in the world would you go to Georgetown? Why not Stanford? Why not the University of Arizona?" She started to go on, but he stepped forward and hugged her. She was a small woman and had never seemed to recover from the scare she'd had when he was in the hospital for those many months.

He answered her as honestly as possible. "I can't give you a good reason. I just can't seem to get the idea out of my head that it's the best place for me to go. I've looked into it, and it's an excellent school. I'm sorry it's far from Arizona, but trust me—I'll get home a lot. I'll miss you guys too much not to see you."

His honesty calmed his mother, and she hugged him back, seemingly much relieved. His Dad nodded with grudging acceptance. His senior year and graduation flew by with the crazy pace that time now seemed to have. Before he knew it, he found himself driving his Dad's Lincoln packed with everything he could carry with him to Washington, DC. As he drove away, it occurred to him that amid all the clothes, books, and family keepsakes he hadn't even thought of packing his bat and glove. It made him feel a little funny to realize this, but after a bit he shrugged to himself and merged onto the I-40 east, convinced he was heading where the universe wanted him to go.

Chapter 16

Washington was a busy city, and very expensive to live in. Danny found a small room a few miles from the medical school and rode the metro every day to avoid the perils of trying to find a parking space. He lived in an area which he heard described as "bad", but to him seemed to be full of a lot of people just working hard to get by. His apartment was over a small Chinese restaurant, and it wasn't long before, when he called the restaurant on his way home each day, they only had to hear his voice to know what to prepare for him. His neighborhood was not exactly scenic, but he grew to love it.

The medical school was big, and full of tradition. His classmates were a good mix of all types of people, and all dedicated and smart. He missed his family at times, but the work swept him up and there never seemed to be enough time to keep up with the crushing study load. He would squeeze in an occasional workout at the university gym, but his bat and glove never made the journey from Arizona to join him. Occasionally his college baseball career would come up, but he would immediately downplay it and soon the conversation moved on. He made few friends but was well thought of and respected as a serious student.

The fall and winter semesters passed quickly, with the experiences blurring into each other. Certain first experiences were memorable for the effect they had on him. He could feel himself become a little queasy when he stood over his first cadaver in Anatomy; he felt a moment of wooziness when the scalp was opened and the drill applied to the skull in his first craniotomy; and he approached his first physical exam on a sick person with grave seriousness. However, every day confirmed that he'd made the right choice. Every class, every experience, everything he did reassured him that he should be doing nothing else.

He visited his parents at Christmas and listened to them both fret intermittently that he needed to socialize more and get out to relax occasionally—maybe even get a girlfriend. He had learned to simply smile and repeat that he'd get around to it when he had a bit more time. The familiar warm Phoenix December was like an old friend, but when he returned to D.C. the bitter eastern winter nearly froze him to death. January and February were paralyzingly frigid, and he trudged back and forth through the snow every day praying for springtime. He continued to love every minute of school, and the course material seemed to stay with him like a language he'd always been destined to learn.

Finally, it was late March and the weather warmed. The plants began to bloom, and he enjoyed the sights and smells of springtime like never before. The winter semester ended in early May, and he signed up for a couple of summer seminars and a surgical observation course, along with a few hours daily in a research lab. He'd meant to stay busy, but even after these arrangements he found himself with time on his hands, to the point of even feeling bored.

Springtime wore on, and one weekend he realized with some surprise that he'd seen none of the city outside of the university. Taking his backpack, he boarded the metro train with the intention of going wherever it took him. Danny found himself on the Green line, speeding under the city. It was early afternoon and a beautiful day. He listened to the recorded voice recite the upcoming stops, waiting for one that sounded intriguing. Finally, he heard the recorded announcement for "Navy Yard-Ballpark Station." Danny looked up, and as the doors opened a feeling he hadn't felt for years came over him. He wanted to watch a ball game. It was surprising, since he often went for days without thinking about baseball, not checking box scores, not watching anything on televisions, and not discussing anything remotely related to sports. However, Danny couldn't deny this powerful urge to see a ballpark.

As he approached the door to exit the train car, he noticed something which made him look twice. He glanced at his reflection in the subway window and saw as if for the first time the reflection of the young man he'd seen years ago in the town he'd dreamed of while in a coma. It was eerie how he looked exactly the same as he'd dreamed all of those years ago. As he left the train, he wondered how he might have seen himself as an adult so accurately when he'd been a 14-year-old boy with a severe brain injury.

He took the stairs up to the street and strolled down the block toward the stadium. As he approached the ballpark, the stadium noises seemed sharper than he recalled, and the loudspeaker announcements echoed through the neighborhood in front of him. He stopped in front of the stadium and took it all in. The bright red signs and roof matched the jerseys worn by most of the fans streaming in. While he hadn't felt as if he missed baseball, it felt good to be there. Danny looked at his phone to check the schedule and saw indeed that they were playing a Saturday afternoon game. Against the Dodgers.

The sight of his old favorite team on the schedule made him smile. He looked up at the gate.

Sold Out, said the signs above the ticket booths. His heart sunk a little, and he turned disappointedly to walk back to the metro station. As he started to walk, he bumped into a woman wearing a Dodgers hat and large, square sunglasses.

"Well, excuse me, handsome," said the woman, in a playful, brassy tone. Something about her voice was familiar, but he couldn't place her. She wore a t-shirt displaying a barroom ad, fronted by two swinging saloon doors. She had on tight pants in a leopard skin pattern.

"Pardon me," he apologized, and kept walking.

"Hey!" She called to his back. It was a commanding voice, and the tone made him stop and turn. She continued: "Are you trying to get into the game?"

"Not really," he said. He was beginning to worry about interacting too much with this woman. Everything about her was loud, and the strange familiarity he felt bothered him.

She stepped closer and put her face closer to his. "Yes, you are. I could see it a mile away."

She reached in her matching leopard skin purse and pulled out a ticket.

"I've got an extra. Take it and go. Knock yourself out." She paused after saying this and then added somewhat

more thoughtfully, "Or maybe don't knock yourself out."
Oddly, she then leaned forward and punched him hard in his
left arm, apparently deliberately avoiding his throwing arm.
He drew back in surprise and rubbed the rapidly forming
bruise. Before he could speak, she turned on her heel and
disappeared into the crowded street. "Thank you," he called
as he gingerly rubbed the sore spot.

He looked at the ticket and walked across the street to
the main gate. After the security check, he wandered the
concourse looking for his aisle and seat. He could see from
the ticket that it was on the field level. He marveled at how
lucky he was to score such a great seat from such a crazy
lady. Finally, he found his aisle, and at the end of the first
inning walked down to the row indicated by his ticket. His
ticket placed him in a seat bordering the aisle and was the
only empty one in the section. The seat next to his was
occupied by an older, tall man who clearly was having
trouble getting enough legroom. He was bearded and wore
large, dark sunglasses against the early afternoon glare. He
was wearing a Dodgers hat.

Danny sat down next to him. The Dodgers took the
field and began a brief warm up. He noticed the man next to
him also appeared to have come alone. He turned to the man
and said,

"I like your hat." The man nodded silently and smiled slightly. After not getting a response, he tried to strike up a conversation again. "I don't imagine you see a lot of Dodger hats in this town." The man continued to watch the field, and Danny gave up trying to make conversation and turned back to the game.

After a moment, he heard the man finally reply.

"One of my best friends was a big Dodger fan. I guess it's a little difficult to give up rooting for those boys once you get interested." He chuckled for a moment and went on. "I'm not sure they want an old coot like me yelling at them."

Danny felt a shock run down his spine. He started to turn back slowly to the man, who was now leaning forward and reaching under his seat. The man brought out a small paper sack and held it out to Danny.

"I've brought an extra hot dog. Would you care for it?"

He held a small brown paper sack out to Danny, who took it. The bag was still warm. He turned the back around and looked at the printing on the front. *Ebbets Field*, it said. His jaw dropped.

"Abe?", he asked.

The older man took off his sunglasses, and Danny knew it was him. Older, craggier, and with more wrinkles, but still him. He leaned forward. He suddenly felt short of breath and a little dizzy. The feeling passed after a few breaths and he steadied himself. He opened the sack. Inside was a perfectly fresh hot dog, with only ketchup on it. He could feel a few people in surrounding seats staring at him, but he didn't care. He raised from his seat and leaned towards Abe, hugging him.

He sat back down, stammered a bit, and tried to speak. "It's so good to see you again. All of these years I thought it was a dream." He paused and tried to ask as diplomatically as possible. "You look… older."

Abe smiled. "I'm not sure why. I don't feel any different. I just look like I did the last time I was here." He shook his head. "Speaking of here, I can't believe how this world has changed. I mostly go in and out for a brief few moments, but what I see amazes me."

Suddenly Danny felt ravenously hungry. He took the hot dog out of the bag and took a bite. It was spicy and delicious. "How did this get here?"

"Jacob gave it to me to pass to you. He said you'd asked for it."

Danny was still in shock. "Was that Calamity in front of the stadium? Did she give me the ticket?"

Abe nodded. "You know she's impossible to reason with once she fixes herself on something, and she wanted to see you."

"I couldn't tell for sure until she hit me."

"Actually, we've all been able to see you over time. The whole town has watched all your games over the years. I'm not sure how we were able to do it, but it looked a lot like the moving pictures on the big scoreboard over there."

He pointed at the scoreboard. "We don't have anything like this at Ebbets Field. You know, we play still play games there against some awfully interesting teams. Last week, we found out how hard that Dizzy Dean fellow can throw the ball, and there's a player named DiMaggio who is very tough to put out."

Danny was silent but couldn't help imagining those players up against his friends. Abe went on. "There were a lot of tears when we watched you play your last game in college, but all of us are excited to follow your medical career. I've known some great doctors in my day, but I think you'll be head and shoulders above them all. You've got a town full of people who'd love to be your patients."

Flustered at the praise, Danny replied modestly. "I think I have to graduate from medical school first."

Abe sat back and folded his arms. The sun was bright, and he put his sunglasses back on.

"I was hesitant to bother Jacob, but I asked if I could talk to you. I need a favor and am hoping you'd be willing to help me out."

"You know I would", said Danny. "Anything." As he said it, he realized how much he'd missed the friendship he'd felt with the tall young man he met long ago. The more he sat with his old friend, the easier it was to also picture him as the muscular young man chopping the tree outside of his cabin.

Abe swallowed, hesitated, and then explained. "My children were very dear to me. After I left here, my biggest regret was that I couldn't be a father to my family. Before we met, I'd never been able to learn anything about my family and those who followed me. We're scattered far and wide." He adjusted his hat, shifted in his seat, and continued to speak quietly.

"I've become aware that there's a boy living in this town that is my grandson, although far, far down the line. He's not aware we're related. Things aren't going well for him. I've learned to look in on him through the same screen we've watched you on, and my heart aches for that boy. It seems that he needs something in his life, and I've thought about it a lot. He could use a friend— maybe even one who will teach him to play ball. Would you do that? I can't do anything for any of the people I remember from my day, but I'd sure like to help him."

Danny noticed that while he was speaking that he heard the same tired, sad voice Lincoln had used when they first met and Danny had told what happened to him.

"Where does he live?"

"I believe he may live pretty close to you. I think if you look for some ball games in your neighborhood, you might find him. His name is Todd. I think that name has come down through the ages from my Mary."

Danny started to protest that he'd need more information, but realized that he was probably being told everything he needed to know. After all, Abe had found Danny without any problem.

"I can't wait to meet him."

"Thank you," said Abe. "I think he might be actually playing today. His mother put him in a league, but he doesn't like it very much. He's all arms and legs, and not exactly a gazelle when he runs."

Danny had a feeling Abe would be gone soon. "Can we watch a little of this game?"

"I can't stay long. Jacob was very reluctant to let me see you. He kept making the point that me coming here was one of the ways that mix-ups like the one that sent you to us happen. It upsets the universe. I don't know when it will move me back, but I feel it will be soon. I hope to see you again, though. I still get melancholy when I get up and realize you've moved on. I hope you don't mind me saying that I've missed you terribly."

"I feel the same", Danny admitted, "It's been a long time since I've had a morning as good as the ones we'd have when we'd pick up pastries and walk to the ball field." After this, Danny became curious. "Speaking of mix-ups, did Daniel Boone ever show up?"

With this question, Abe's mood seemed to lighten immediately. He laughed. "Well, that's a story in itself. Jacob said that when they found him, he was far away back in the ancient early times, wearing an outfit fashioned from animal skins. Apparently, he'd made himself king of several tribes of men from those times and didn't want to leave. They hunt, fish, and battle all sorts of strange creatures. So, your little house next to mine is still vacant."

The thought of his home near Abe's made him homesick for his friends.

"Well," he said, "When the time comes there's nowhere I'd rather be."

Obviously touched, Abe put his hand on Danny's shoulder. "I'd like that. But you've got some work to do here first." He looked at the scoreboard. "I've got to go, but first let's watch the Dodger third baseman at bat. With that long red beard, he reminds me of some of the Union soldiers I used to see march down Pennsylvania Avenue."

The third baseman came up. He took his stance, and as the pitch came, he drew his left leg up and leaned into the ball, making solid contact. With the crack of the bat, Danny could tell that this was a home run. He jumped to his feet and strained to look over the people standing in front of him to watch the ball sail over the left field fence. He yelled and cheered enthusiastically, then turned to see Abe's reaction.

The seat was empty, and Abe was gone.

Chapter 17

Danny watched the rest of the second inning and the third as well, then began to feel restless. He was experiencing an overwhelmingly strong feeling that the last several years had been more of a dream than he'd had when he was comatose. Everything he'd been through since waking up from his head injury seemed rushed and hazy; memories and feelings of the time he spent in his little town rushed back into his head fresh and alive. He looked out at the field and wished Abe were still there. He already missed his friend. He walked up the stairs to a souvenir stand on the concourse and bought a Dodgers hat, then left the stadium.

Danny traveled home, but when his apartment came into view, instead of going in, he passed the Chinese restaurant and continued walking. He strolled aimlessly for another 20 minutes and stopped at a corner market for a soft drink. As he paid for his Coke, he heard shouts and cheers drift through the screen door. He peered through the window and saw a patch of green across the street, next to a post office.

"Is that a park?" He asked the elderly man behind the counter.

"That's Postville park," said the store owner. "The kids play ball there. I don't know the real name of the field. We call it that because of the post office over there."

At this point, Danny wasn't surprised that the park shared the same name as the little park in Springfield where Abe had played townball growing up. He knew it was exactly where he was supposed to go. Sipping his drink, he crossed the street at the corner and walked to the park. There was a Little League game in progress. The kids appeared to be around 12 years old and wore uniforms that bore the names of local businesses sponsors. *Frank Ruiz Barber Shop* was on the field wearing green uniforms with yellow stockings, while the *Max Andeweg Insurance* team was up to bat wearing gray with orange stockings. A small group of benches were on the third base side of the field with just a few spectators and plenty of room left to sit.

He sat down on a bench and looked over the team on the field. It was a typical group of kids of all sizes, and no one stood out. He inspected the Max Andeweg team, who looked much the same. His gaze wandered to the few kids not playing and riding the bench in the Frank Ruiz dugout. He saw one young player get up and wander to the edge.

This kid caught his eye. He was tall for a 12-year-old, though his green uniform looked at least a size too large.

He moved in a loose, uncertain way, and clearly was not having any fun. As the boy walked around the fenced-in area, it looked like he was trying to escape. When he turned and Danny saw his long, thin nose and angular face with a prominent jaw, there was no doubt of a family resemblance. The unhappy player looked exactly like a 12-year-old version of Abe, and the look on the boy's face reminded Danny of when he first saw his friend, unhappily chopping at the tree by his house. Danny marveled at the never-ending chain of coincidences.

The game wore on. The Frank Ruiz team was getting beaten. Badly. In the seventh inning, they were down 9-1. Occasionally, one of the parents on the sidelines would shout words of encouragement, but it was mostly quiet. In the bottom of the seventh, the coach motioned to the boy Danny had noticed and pointed to right field. The boy nodded and with obvious reluctance, picked up his glove and trotted out to right field, where he stood and watched the other boys warm up. Nobody threw the ball to him.

The first batter walked. The next batter was a big, left-handed kid who promptly hit a fly ball to right field. Danny watched the young Abe look-alike move clumsily under the ball, misjudge it, and at the last minute have it bounce off his glove and roll far behind him. The center fielder had come over to back him up, clearly expecting the error. He picked up the ball and threw it in, but it was too late to stop the lead runner from scoring and the batter reaching third base. The kid in right field stared at the ground. He looked miserable.

The next inning, the boy came up to bat. He hung back in the batter's box and flinched at every pitch. He managed only one weak swing during the whole at-bat, and struck out almost immediately. He stumbled back to the dugout, red-faced and awkward.

Danny watched the rest of the game. There were no more hits to right field, and the kid never got to bat again. His team ended up losing 10-1. When the game ended, the coach had the boys gather around him. He said a few quiet words and tried to encourage every boy. Danny watched the clumsy boy stand at the back of the group. He wasn't listening and kept looking toward the parking lot. No car appeared to be waiting for him.

The team scattered, and the coach began to gather the equipment and place it in a large duffel bag. Danny walked over.

"Excuse me," he asked the Coach. The man turned toward him.

"What can I help you with? He asked.

"My name is Danny Boone. I go to medical school at Georgetown and live a few blocks away. I played ball for four years at ASU and have really been missing the game lately. I noticed you didn't have any assistants. I know it sounds a little crazy, but I was wondering if I could help with coaching."

The coach hesitated. Danny added, "I'll also be happy to pick up the gear after every game and practice." This made the other man smile. After another moment, he put out his hand.

"John Lloyd", he said, shaking Danny's hand with a powerful grip. "I played some ball myself, back in the day."

At this point, Danny felt as if it would be better not to ask if he was connected to the great John Henry Lloyd. Every time he turned around there seemed to be another weird crossover from his dream to what he now hoped was reality. He'd had enough surprises for the day, and just decided to stop asking.

Lloyd continued. "If you give me your e-mail, I can forward you an application to send back to the league. They'll need a couple of days to process it, but it should be done by our next practice on Wednesday."

"Thanks," said Danny.

"No problem," said the coach. "Practice is at five."

"You know," he tilted his head slightly. "You look a little familiar. Have we ever played against each other?"

"Maybe in another life," replied Danny, and they both laughed. He helped pick up the gear and then called in an order for Chinese food. It had been a crazy day, and he didn't feel like cooking.

Chapter 18

After a couple of phone calls, the league cleared Danny to coach. When Wednesday came, Danny walked over to the park. Most of the team was already warming up, but he didn't see the boy he'd watched so carefully the other day. Finally, as practice started, an older car which might have been generously described as a wreck pulled up, and the boy got out slowly. He had a brief conversation with the woman driving as he was leaving the car. It appeared he was losing an argument not to go to practice. He heard the woman raise her voice just loud enough for Danny to hear her say: "You need to do something, and you need to make some friends." The kid hung his head and trudged to the field.

Danny walked over to greet him wearing a glove he'd just bought. It felt good.

"Hi," he greeted the unenthusiastic boy. "I'm a new assistant to Coach Lloyd. I'm Danny."

The skinny boy looked him over, and then managed a barely audible hello.

"What's your name?' Danny asked.

"Todd," replied the boy. "Todd Weaver."

"Do you like baseball?" Danny was pretty certain of the response he'd get.

"Not really. My Mom makes me play. She says I need to make friends and get outside." He looked around morosely. "I don't think I'm making any friends," he confessed.

"Well," said Danny. "You've just made one." He reached in his pocket and pulled out a ball. "Why don't we warm up over on the first base side?"

After walking to the spot, the boy tried to throw Danny the ball. He was a right-hander, but led with the wrong foot when he threw and almost fell over. The throw went wild, and the boy waited for Danny to scold him.

Instead, Danny nodded and pointed to Todd's arms. "With long arms like that, we'll have you throwing the ball like it's coming out of a cannon. We just need to tune up your footwork. When you throw, rock back a little on your right foot, then step into the throw with your left foot."

He threw the ball slowly and right at the boy's glove, and Todd managed to catch it.

"Nice," said Danny. "You catch like a natural."

He could see that even that small amount of praise gave the boy confidence, and after a few more attempts he was able to throw with more power and even a little speed.

"What grade are you in?" Danny asked as they continued to play catch.

"Seventh," replied the boy. "My Mom and I live by my school close to the park. She is the manager for the Jack in the Box across the street. She's worked there for 10 years."

"I love Jack in the Box," said Danny. "Who doesn't like a sourdough bacon cheeseburger?"

Todd started to brighten a little. "I love the mini-tacos. My Mom brings me those and an Oreo milkshake sometimes when she comes home."

"Does your Dad live around here?" Danny asked. The boy slowed his throw for a second.

"He died. He was a soldier in Afghanistan and got shot when I was 7."

Danny caught the ball and held it for a moment. "I'm sorry," he said. "I'm grateful that he was fighting for our country. I'm sure you are proud of him."

"I'm mostly just sad when I think about it, but I am proud, too."

Danny tried to turn the focus back to baseball. "I think he'd be pretty happy with the way you are throwing. You've already improved so much." Todd seemed to stand a little taller after each compliment. Danny continued. "I'm going to throw a couple of fly balls to you. Back up a little."

Todd moved back and looked uncertain, but it was clear he had already gained some confidence. Danny threw the ball in a high arc, and Todd completely misjudged the toss. It went over his head, and he sighed and turned to run after the ball. When he picked it up, he threw the ball back to Danny with a defeated air.

Danny caught it and paused. "Don't be too hard on yourself. Fly balls are tough, but everything gets better with practice."

He threw a several more, and by the time he finished, Todd had caught two in the air and was looking proud. Coach Lloyd called the team in and split the squad up for a practice game. Danny grimaced when he watched Todd strike out twice, and had to stop himself from cheering when the teams changed sides and Todd caught a shallow fly ball. Danny felt that was decent progress, and told Todd so at the end of the game. Danny could tell from the mix of gratitude and embarrassment that the boy wasn't used to hearing positive comments.

True to his word, Danny gathered the gear at the end of practice. He watched as Todd waited for his mother, but when he had finished and was ready to leave, the boy was still sitting by himself, waiting. Dusk was approaching, and the park was empty. He walked over to the boy.

"Waiting for your ride?"

As Todd nodded, his angular features reminded Danny again of how much he looked like Abe.

"Sometimes my Mom runs late because somebody calls in sick at work. She doesn't like me to walk home alone, so I wait for her."

Danny sat down by him. "She sounds like a pretty smart Mom. You're a big kid, but it pays to be careful."

They talked for a few minutes more. Motioning toward the field, Danny spoke again. "You really looked much better out there today."

"Yeah, but I still can't hit."

"I'll bet we can help that. It just takes practice, and it should be fun. I played baseball for many years, and I can tell you that as we work at it, you'll start to like it more. Especially when you start to get some hits."

Just then Todd's Mom pulled up and came to a stop nearby. The engine rumbled and pinged. Danny walked Todd over to the car.

He approached the driver's side, and she smiled and rolled the window down to speak with him. She appeared about forty, and was wearing a Jack in the Box logo visor with a matching logo on her shirt. Her hair was pulled back in a ponytail, and although she looked tired, she seemed friendly. A light breeze started to blow as Danny stood near the window.

"Hi," she said, extending her hand. "I'm Mary. Are you Todd's coach?"

Danny shook her hand. "I'm the assistant coach, actually. I'm Danny Boone. I live near here and used to play ball in college. I miss the game, so I asked Coach Lloyd if I could volunteer. I just got my application approved."

She smiled. "How nice of you to help. And thanks for waiting with Todd. I get off work late sometimes since I manage the restaurant, and I don't like him to walk home alone."

"It's a pleasure. He's a great kid. He reminds me a lot of a younger version of my best friend." He surprised himself as he realized that of all the friendships he had throughout his life so far, the man he hadn't seen for years and until

Saturday thought was a dream was actually his best and most trusted friend.

"You think so?" She was clearly happy to hear that. Todd settled into the passenger seat and buckled in. "I keep telling Todd he needs to get outdoors and meet some kids. Since we lost his Dad, he's really turned inward."

"Mom." Todd clearly didn't want to be the topic of conversation.

She turned to him. "Sorry, honey. I just love you so much and want you to blossom. You are the best kid I know!"

Todd reddened and looked down in his lap. This was one mother who wasn't going to give up on her boy.

After a moment of silence, Danny said: "Anytime you're late I'm happy to walk Todd home. I can use the exercise and I don't live far."

She sighed with relief. "I would appreciate that so much. I worry about him here waiting for me."

"No problem. You can count on it."

She drove away, and from the looks of it, Danny thought she was probably again telling Todd what a good idea it was to play Little League. He could see the boy staring at the window. Surprisingly, as they turned the corner, Todd looked up and waved to Danny, and on his face was the start of a smile.

Danny spent the next couple of days in the lab and attending various seminars. On Saturday, he went back to practice. Even though he had agreed to this as a favor to Abe, he had to admit to himself that he had looked forward to practice more than anything else all week.

On Saturday, the team had a bye, so they held a practice session instead. As Danny walked on the field, he saw Todd warming up and playing catch with another, smaller boy. Todd was still a bit tentative in his throwing, but was becoming more accurate and catching the ball almost every time. It was a huge improvement.

The coach called the team together and practice began. After some basic fielding and batting drills, they divided up and had a practice game. Todd was in right field again, but nobody hit to him. Still, it looked to Danny like he actually wanted to get a chance to field the ball. He was not as confident at bat, however, and struck out twice.

Practice ended, and Todd approached Danny.

"Hi."

"Hello there," replied Danny.

"Can you walk home with me? It's only 4, and my Mom won't be home until 6."

"Sure," said Danny. "But if you're not in a hurry, how about we do a little batting practice? I was watching you bat, and while you didn't get a hit, you have a nice swing. I'll bet you're this close to consistently hitting the ball."

"Really?" Todd asked with a hint of disbelief.

"No kidding," said Danny reassuringly. "You remind me of this friend I had. He used to chop wood, and when he swung a baseball bat, he looked a lot like you. With just a little practice, he could hit the ball a mile."

They walked back to the diamond, which was empty. There was still plenty of afternoon sun left. They picked out a bat, and Danny showed Todd a basic grip. At the plate, he demonstrated a stance.

"A lot of people don't realize it, but you don't hit with your arms or even the bat. You hit with your eyes."

Todd looked puzzled. "What do you mean?"

"If you look at pictures of the greatest hitters when they hit the ball, they're not looking at the field. They're focused on seeing the ball hit the bat. Always watch the ball approach and connect with your bat, and you'll get some solid hits."

Danny walked to the mound and turned to face the plate. "Okay. Here come some easy ones. Just take your time."

After a few pitches, Todd started to foul a few off. Finally, he connected and a sure single landed in shallow left field. He laughed and took a couple of quick practice swings.

"Feels good, right?" Danny asked. Todd nodded enthusiastically and took his stance. He hit he next one as well, and things continued to improve slowly over the next hour. Danny picked up the speed on the pitches, and Todd kept hitting. They'd stop occasionally and pick up the balls. They told each other dumb jokes while gathering them up, and then started a little mild trash talking.

While walking home, Todd spoke about life in general and how he didn't like school. He seemed to be much more comfortable the more they chatted. They rounded a corner and went up the sidewalk of an older, small, white house. The yard was overgrown with weeds. Danny looked at Todd, who was clearly self-conscious about the appearance of his home.

"Our house is pretty run down, but Mom and I keep it clean on the inside. She says we're going to live simply so we can save up money for my college."

"What do you want to study?", asked Danny.

"It sounds crazy," said Todd, "but I think I want to be a lawyer."

Danny smiled. "So did my friend who looks like you," Danny said. "For some reason I'm not surprised."

Chapter 19

The Frank Ruiz squad lost the next game, but not by as much. With Danny as an assistant, Coach Lloyd had been able to spend more time with each boy while Danny worked with the rest. The extra practice showed, and the team was definitely playing better ball. The whole team was improving and enjoying the game more. Danny continued to work with Todd over the next several weeks, and they'd usually walk home together. During these walks Danny got to know the boy a little better each time.

Todd was a serious kid, mostly because he felt awkward around people. He gradually displayed a great deal of intelligence and even a sense of humor over time. He was also scrupulously honest. After a couple of weeks, Todd's mother invited Danny to dinner. Danny went to their house, and while at dinner, Todd opened up even more and related some memories of his father. It was the first time Danny heard him speak about his Dad. Danny followed this by telling a few funny baseball stories from his own career in college, and then Todd asked, "Who are your heroes?"

Danny started to speak, but Todd cut him off. "Besides baseball players, I mean."

"I wasn't going to name a baseball player," said Danny. "When I'm not in class studying medicine, I like to read about historical figures."

"Who are your favorites?", Todd asked him.

"Well", Danny replied thoughtfully, "I like to read about different people. I just finished a book on Napoleon. I want to go to the National Museum of African American History and Culture to learn what I can about Fredrick Douglass and a woman civil war soldier, Cathay Williams. I like to read about the old west, about the history of South America, and other stuff."

"Yeah," said Todd, "but who is your very favorite?"

"It would have to be Abraham Lincoln," said Danny. "He was a great man and had a terrific sense of humor. He seems like he'd be a good friend."

Todd's mother, Mary, gasped. "That's so weird. There's a legend in my mother's family that somehow we are descended from Lincoln, although nobody can explain how. That's how Todd got his name. He's actually named Robert Todd Weaver. A lot of Lincoln's family have carried those names over the years. My husband and I heard about this and wanted to work that name into our family. We figured if we were wrong, he was still the greatest American of all time."

"I'm sure if Abe knew about that he'd be tickled," said Danny.

"You talk like you know him," laughed Mary. "Did he like to be called Abe?"

"I think so," said Danny. "I'll guess I'll have to ask him next time I talk to him!"

The three of them laughed again. Danny had dessert, and then got up to go. As he was in the entry way putting on his jacket, Todd's mother motioned to him. Dan paused as she walked up to him.

"I have to thank you."

Danny was puzzled. "For what?"

Mary smiled. "For everything. Todd is like a different kid. He used to hate baseball; now he loves it. He didn't have any friends at school, and now he is buddies with the guys on his team. He seems happier and is even studying more. He used to sit home alone all the time. Now his friends will call and come over. It's almost too good to be true."

"I don't have anything to do with it," Danny said. "He's a terrific kid, and you're a great Mom. It's a privilege to get to work with him."

She flushed red from the praise and looked at the ground. Then, looking up again, she spoke.

"You can be modest, but it seems like meeting you has been the only good thing that's happened to him since his Dad died. He's such a smart and sensitive kid, and I was watching him wither right in front of me no matter what I tried. Being on your team has really helped him to blossom."

"It's not my team," Danny said modestly. "Coach Lloyd deserves all the credit. I just help out. He's a good coach."

"I'm glad you help him. I worry about Todd so much. We barely get by on what I earn and his Dad's survivor benefits. There's so much more I'd like to do for him. But making friends and having people like you in his life compensates for almost everything."

"Well, I'll be around for quite a while, and I'm looking forward to watching him grow up. I think he's got talents we barely know anything about, and baseball will probably be the least of them."

With that, he said goodnight and left their house. It was past nine, and the streets were almost empty. A slight fog made the streetlights flicker, and the stars were hidden. Shadows fell and moved across the cracked sidewalks with the breeze. He turned the last corner before his home and saw a tall figure sitting on a bus bench, reading a newspaper under a flickering light. The man wore a long black coat and wore wire-framed reading glasses.

Danny walked toward the figure sitting on the bench. The man turned a page and shook his head.

"Newspapers today aren't any better than they were in my day. As a matter of fact, they seem worse. You can't tell who's reporting and who's just complaining. This *Post* must be new since I was here, and it's terrible. They don't seem to like America very much." He laughed. "Although, I must admit, I do like the comics."

Danny was glad to see Abe. "Your great- however many times-great-grandson is a fantastic young man. He reminds me a lot of you."

Abe looked at the streetlight. "These lights are beautiful." He was quiet for a moment and continued. "I am indebted to you. He seems so much happier, and I believe we share an affinity for your game."

"He can't hit like you yet," said Danny. "But he's improving. I may have him lift some weights in the off-season to build up his upper body strength. He can't just go around chopping down trees every day, like some people."

Abe laughed again. "Too bad. It can be very therapeutic." He turned to look at Danny, who couldn't help again noticing the lines of worry and wear on Abe's face.

Before Abe could speak again, Danny broke in. "You walked a pretty tough road on this earth, didn't you?"

Abe nodded without speaking. Danny went on. "You don't just look older than when we were neighbors. You look like you've carried the whole world on your shoulders for years."

"It does tend to age you," Abe admitted. "However, I do feel good about the fact that the republic is together." He continued. "I'd like to head over to the ball field and see if your throwing arm has gotten any better, but they won't give me much time."

"We may yet get a chance to do that," said Danny.

Abe nodded in agreement and said: "Over time and since meeting you, I've come to learn to expect the unexpected. There is, though, another thing I'd like you to do."

"Okay," said Danny. "What?"

"I worry about the boy and his mother. She works hard, but they hardly have an ear of corn some nights for food." He was quiet for a second, and then added, "I'm sure you've figured out that he's the last of my bloodline, and some nights, I worry they'll starve."

"I understand that you're concerned about them." Danny felt bad to see his friend worry. "I can take out another student loan and give that to them," he suggested.

Abe smiled in gratitude. "You were a fine boy and are a good man. I appreciate your offer, but over time they'll need more than you can gain through a loan."

He went on. "I'd like you to take the boy shopping. He's saved a few dollars, and his Mother's birthday is coming up. Take him out to some of the secondhand shops down the street." He gestured to the row of antique stores down the block. "He may find something nice for her."

"Sure", said Danny. "Now, is this about the time you mysteriously vanish?"

Abe playfully wagged a finger at him. "That's not my doing. You know very well they move you around when they want to."

Danny grinned. "Don't be so sensitive. Are you telling me that Abe Lincoln can't take a little ribbing from a friend?"

Abe shook his head and grinned back. "I can take a ribbing, but you're right that I'm bothered. I admit to being a little pastier-faced than usual, though, but maybe because I hate to go so soon. I can feel it starting even now."

Danny remembered the beeping and chiming he heard while playing those last innings at Ebbets field. "I know. It's a bit eerie." He put his hand on Abe's shoulder. "It was good to see you again."

He turned away slowly, in spite of wanting to stretch the moment out before his friend was gone. He walked down the sidewalk for a minute or two and looked back. The mist made a ghostly halo around the streetlight, and the empty bench shimmered a bit like a mirage in the Arizona desert.

Chapter 20

Several more weeks of the season passed. The day of the last game for the Frank Ruiz team finally arrived. Due to their improving play, the team had moved up considerably from last place in the league standings. They were now tied for second place but had no real chance to win the league title. However, they now unofficially led the league with respect to how much fun they were having with each game. Coach Lloyd was smart, supportive, and knew just how to motivate the boys. Danny would add his support in any way he could, and together the two of them made sure that if the boys didn't win, they still had fun and felt good about themselves and the game. Jokes were told, pranks were played (mainly on the coaches), and boisterous chants and cheering were heard nonstop from the dugout.

As it happened, the last game was again played against the first team Danny had seen them play: Max Andeweg Insurance. They were the first-place team and were very strong. The previous game had ended with an 11-1 loss for Frank Ruiz, and it was still very fresh in the minds of the boys.

Todd had finally won a starting position on the team, and usually would play at least seven innings in the outfield. He was getting one or two hits per game, and occasionally showing power with a double or triple. Teams who had seen him play earlier in the season had a hard time believing he was the same player, and those who took him lightly quickly learned he could hit and field well enough to win a game. He was still gangly, but now moved with confidence and determination.

It was another Saturday afternoon, and the weather was getting warm and humid. Mary had the day off and came out to watch the game. The benches were almost completely full of enthusiastic parents. It was a big change from the first game, when most of the seats had been empty. Danny was coaching third base, and John Lloyd ran the dugout and coached first base. Todd was batting sixth, and came up in the second inning with his team down by 2. He drove in a run with a hard single to left field, and then surprised both teams by stealing second. He scored on another single by the next batter, and things were tied.

Danny played left field and was covering the territory much better. In the fourth inning, a Max Andeweg runner walked and was on first when the next batter hit a short blooper to left. The third base coach had seen Todd play previously and assumed there'd be an error. He waved the runner from first around to third, but was surprised when Todd scooped up the ball on the second bounce and fired a perfect throw to third. The runner was an easy out. Mary stood up and clapped, and Danny had to try to restrain himself from cheering too loudly.

The innings wore on, and finally it was the bottom of the ninth. The score was tied at 6-6, and the Max Andeweg team was up. They quickly put runners on second and third with no outs, but the next batter hit a pop fly. A strikeout followed, and the next batter came up. He was their cleanup hitter and had already tripled off of the right field fence. After taking a strike, he swung hard at the next pitch and hit a sharp line drive to left field. The ball barely cleared the outstretched arm of the shortstop and started to lose altitude in shallow left field. Todd had done a nice job of anticipating where the ball would go, and started in fast after the ball. For a moment the clumsiness disappeared, and he went for the ball at a full, graceful sprint. He dove for the ball with his glove extended. He stopped the ball, but it wasn't clear if he'd caught the ball or simply trapped it. By reflex, he stood up and threw to third, but the runner had already tagged up and scored.

When the runner crossed the plate, play halted, and all eyes turned toward Todd. If he'd caught the ball on the fly, the Frank Ruiz team would be up next and have a chance to win the game. If he'd trapped the ball, the game was over. The umpire came out from behind home plate and jogged out to left field, where Todd stood waiting. The coaches, including Danny, followed. When they reached left field, the umpire caught his breath and spoke to Todd.

"Nobody was close enough to call the play. Did you catch the ball, son? Was he out?"

It was obvious that Todd understood the situation, and just as obvious that he wanted to win. He paused for a moment, and then replied, "I wished I'd caught the ball, but I trapped it just after it bounced. It was a base hit."

The umpire nodded and turned to the crowd. "Game over!" he shouted. There was a sigh from the Frank Ruiz spectators, followed by loud cheers for the boys as they jogged in.

Danny watched Todd run in and was pleased to see almost every player run up to him, pat his back, and say "Nice try," or "Way to play honest." It was evident that Todd wasn't sure what to expect, but he clearly appreciated the support. Danny beamed with pride. The kid was certainly a

Lincoln and had just shown a measure of integrity worthy of his ancestor.

The boys gathered for a rousing post-game talk by John Lloyd. He congratulated each boy for their play and sportsmanship and emphasized again that the game should always be fun. At the end, the boys cheered and high-fived. Several talked to Todd about playing a pickup game at the park on the following Saturday.

As the field cleared, Danny again began to gather the equipment. Mary came over and thanked Danny for his coaching work with Todd. Danny stopped and held the bag for a moment.

"I appreciate you saying that, but you're the one who needs to be thanked. You are doing a great job of raising that kid. I think he's going to be a real leader someday, and he owes it all to the kind of mother he has."

She was a little uncomfortable with the praise, and replied, "Well, he didn't start to come out of his shell until you showed up. For some reason, playing ball has really helped him to shine like I always felt he could."

"It's a game that seems to have all sorts of powers," laughed Danny. "You'd be surprised what can happen with it."

"I can't argue with results," Mary agreed.

"By the way," said Danny, "Todd wants to have me walk with him to do a little shopping today for your birthday, which is rumored to be today. Can I bring him home a little later? We were just going to look around the neighborhood."

Mary was embarrassed. "That's right. My 29th is here-again." She smiled disarmingly and continued.

"You're lucky I'm turning forty and you're in your twenties or I'd be chasing you all over the city."

Now Danny was embarrassed. Mary laughed and tapped his arm. "Don't worry, you're safe." Then she wrinkled her brow a little and asked, "I wonder sometimes, though, how a good-looking doctor-to-be like you doesn't have anybody special."

Danny started to stammer, then cleared his throat. "There was—a long time ago. We kind of got separated."

"Too bad," said Mary. "Her loss."

"Actually, it was both our losses. But there was no way around it."

"Well, you're young," said Mary. "You never know."

Danny shook his head. "You have no idea how much I agree there."

She said goodbye and walked to the car. Todd was waiting on one of the spectator benches. Danny carried the bag over to Coach Lloyd, who put in in the back of his car. He shook Danny's hand.

"It's been a pleasure. It's fun to coach with somebody who loves the game."

"Thanks for letting me help. You're a great coach. You must have been a great player."

Lloyd looked at him with suspicion. "Are you sure we've never played against each other?"

"Pretty sure," said Danny, "but I could be wrong."

The coach gave Danny a knowing smile. "Well, maybe we will sometime. Right?"

Danny remembered what he could of the opposing second baseman at the Ebbets field and realized there did appear to be a strong resemblance.

"I hope so," he said. "I think we could have some fun."

As Lloyd drove away, Danny called to Todd and he came over.

"Well, boss. Where do you want to shop for your Mom?"

Todd looked up and down the street. "I only have twenty-three dollars." Maybe we can try some of the antique and thrift shops over there." He pointed down the avenue toward his home.

They proceeded in the direction of the stores. Once there, Danny noticed a store just down the block that happened to be situated directly behind the bus bench Abe had been sitting on a few weeks before. He read the sign as they were walking: *You'll Find It Here.*

Danny nudged Todd. "How about we take a look over there?" he said, pointing to the store.

Todd shrugged and they walked to the door. They peered through the display window for a moment, and went in. The store appeared deserted and had a musty smell. The inside was deceptively large, and there appeared to be both an upstairs and back room. Table after table and shelf after shelf were packed with old objects: clocks, jewelry, household tools, and broken toys. Most were covered with dust.

Danny looked at Todd, who wrinkled his nose. "I don't know," he said. "This place looks too old."

Just then a strong voice with a British accent came from behind a shelf near the back of the front room.

"Of course it's old, young man. That's what makes everything here even more precious. Most of these things are over 150 years old, and a lot of us think that there hasn't been much accomplished since then." The person speaking came out from behind the shelf, carrying a stack of books. Danny looked at him and then looked again. He appeared to be exactly like a clean-shaven version of the young Charles Dickens. The proprietor looked at Todd and then Danny. His face betrayed no recognition.

He put the books down, along with an old cigar box sitting on top of the stack. "What may I help you find in my old curiosity shop?" he asked.

Todd spoke up, sounding dubious that they would be successful. "We're looking for something for my mother for her birthday."

The man nodded and scratched his chin thoughtfully. "Hmmm. Does she need a clock?" He picked up a warped wood desk clock with a rusted face and no hands.

Todd shook his head. "No."

An old ivory hairbrush, missing most of the bristles, was then offered. "How about a brush?"

"Not that one," said Todd.

He was next presented with a tattered book with broken binding, missing the front cover.

"How about this 1853 King James Bible?"

Todd shook his head and looked at Danny. "I don't think so. Maybe we should try another store."

"Thank you," said Danny, and they turned to leave through the door.

"One moment," said the proprietor. "May I suggest you look upstairs? Some of our better items are kept there." When he said this, he looked directly at Danny.

Danny stopped and shrugged. "We're here," he said to Todd. "We may as well take a look."

Todd looked even more doubtful, but agreed. They walked up a thin, spiral staircase to the second floor. It led to a smaller room, full of even more ramshackle items, mostly appearing to be in bits and pieces. There was one small window. It was almost completely coated with dust, and only a small area the size of a dollar coin let in any light. The effect, though, was that of a small spotlight. Danny followed the solitary beam of light through the shadowy room, and saw it fall on a table at one end of the room. The table was piled high with what could only be described as junk. Sitting on top of the pile and directly illuminated by the beam of light was a small wooden box. It was no bigger than 10 inches long and appeared to be square with respect to its depth and width. While it had many dents and scratches, there was an ornate woodwork design on the top of a horse pulling a carriage. An old latch fastened it shut,.

Danny undid the latch and opened the box. A surprisingly clean red velvet fabric lined the box. He looked at Todd.

"This is really pretty," he said.

Todd nodded. "You're right. She loves jewelry boxes. I think she'd like this one a lot."

They carried the box carefully down the staircase and set it on the counter. The shop owner looked at it and smiled.

"Nice," he said. "I'd bet a million pounds your mother will love it. "

Todd nodded, and then said nervously. "There's no price on it. How much does it cost?"

The man smiled. "How much do you have?"

"I have 23 dollars," said Todd. "That's all I've got."

"Well," said the man, pulling a small abacus from his pocket. "Let's see."

He moved some of the beads on the abacus back and forth, pretending to concentrate. Todd watched anxiously. After a minute or so of this, he looked up and smiled.

"Amazing. That will be just enough."

"Including tax?" Danny asked.

"Most certainly," replied the man. "As a matter of fact, I'll throw in this old cigar box for you, too."

He picked up the box sitting on top of the stack of books on the counter and held it out to Danny.

"Here you go, my friend. Whatever is in there is yours." Danny took the box and thanked the man, and they started to leave the store with Todd clutching the old wooden box.

As the door started to close behind them, he heard the man yell behind them.

"It was good to see you!" And as the door swung closed, Danny thought he heard the word "again" trail off. He turned and looked through the door but saw only the empty shop. He wanted to return, but thought the better of it and kept walking with Todd. They arrived at the house and went inside. They had picked up a gift bag on the way home, and when they went inside there was a small birthday cake on the table in the entry way. The cake was decorated with lettering which said: "Happy Birthday to Me!"

As they laughed at Todd's mother's choice of words, Mary came out of the kitchen, singing *Happy Birthday* to herself. The boys laughed and joined in. They sat down in the kitchen and carried on talking nonstop about the funny things that had happened over the course of the little league season.

They ate their slices of cake. When they finished, Todd shyly reached under the table and handed the bag to his mother, along with a handmade card.

Mary read the card with delight and looked in the gift bag. She exclaimed with delight when she lifted the small box from the bag.

"Todd," she exclaimed, "it's beautiful." She turned the box around to see all sides and rubbed the carved wood carriage on the lid. She opened the lid and admired the red velvet lining. She looked at it for a moment, and then closed the lid and held up the box again.

"There's something odd about this box," she said eyeing it carefully. "It's too shallow inside compared to the outside."

She tapped on the sides and lid of the box, then opened the lid again and tapped on the velvet floor of the box. It sounded hollow compared to the rest of the box. She looked puzzled but was curious. While Danny and Todd watched, she walked to the kitchen and came back with a small paring knife. She stood over the box and pushed the knife down the side where it met the bottom.

They heard a small *crack!* and the floor of the box tilted and started to move. In a moment, the floor was out. She gasped and looked inside the hidden compartment and saw a small stack of old envelopes held together by a neatly tied black ribbon.

Mary handed the box to Danny, and carefully untied the envelopes. The envelopes were not sealed, and she carefully opened the one on top. There was a single word on the outside of the envelope: *Mary*. It was written in a practiced, elegant hand. She removed an aged piece of yellow paper from the envelope and carefully unfolded it. She read in silence for a minute, then gasped and stared at it. She looked away from the letter, and her eyes welled with tears. Without speaking, she handed the letter to Danny with exaggerated care.

Danny took the letter and very carefully examined it. It was dated April 3, 1865 and began with the salutation "Dear Wife." The letter stated in gentle terms that it was being written in case of death and was written as an affirmation of the letter-writer's love. The letter mentioned a "fearful premonition" of death, with the greatest fear being that the writer could lose his loved ones. After reading more tender expressions of love and gratitude, Danny came to the signature. He felt the breath go out of him when he read the name *A. Lincoln*.

They were dumbstruck, and silently looked at the other envelopes. One was addressed to Robert, another to

Tad, another to Billy, one to Joshua, and three others also addressed only by first names.

Finally, they were able to speak. After a brief discussion, they carried the letters and box to a bank a few blocks away which was just about to close. Using Danny's credit card, they rented a large safe deposit box which just fit the wooden box, and securely stored the letters. When they left the bank, Mary broke down again in tears and hugged Todd.

"You're the only gift I ever wanted," she said, "But this is pretty nice. Thank you, honey."

Todd hugged her back and smiled at Danny.

Danny walked them back to their home, and after talking for another hour finally got up to leave. As he said his goodbyes and was walking to the door, Todd picked an object up from a nearby chair and followed him.

"Don't forget your cigar box!" he said lightheartedly. "Maybe it will have some valuable cigars!" They laughed. Danny took the box absent-mindedly and set out for home. As he walked, he spotted a trash can on the sidewalk and approached it to throw the box away. As he started to drop it in, the top fell open and several pieces of paper spilled to the ground. Ever the good citizen, he bent down to pick them up and noticed the first piece was unusually thick. It was about 1

½ inches by 2 ½ inches, and in the growing dusk Danny thought he could make out a picture on one side.

Curious, he turned the light of his phone on the paper. There was old-fashioned printing on one side which said something about a cigarette brand; he flipped the card over and saw a picture which looked vaguely familiar. It was of a young man with a serious expression and hair parted in the middle. As he stared at it, he recognized the shortstop from the visiting team at Ebbets Field. He focused the light closer and read the small caption under the picture: "Wagner, Pittsburgh." He caught his breath sharply and picked up the other small papers which had fallen out of the box. All of them were similar, and the names included Cobb and Lajoie. He shook his head, stood up, and began to walk home, again passing the shop he'd been in earlier that day with Todd. He stopped and shined the light of his phone through the window. The shop was empty, with only bare walls and dust where a store had been earlier in the day.

Chapter 21

The letters produced a national sensation. Mary wisely remained anonymous. She kept the two written to Lincoln's sons, and told Danny she did that because they reminded her of how her husband must have felt about Todd. The rest sold at auction for a combined total of just over 9 million dollars. She sold their home and bought a nicer one a few miles from Danny. The rest of the summer passed quickly, and Danny fell back into his studies. Near the end of the year, he started his clinical rotations and became even busier balancing studies with time on the hospital wards and operating room. When he could get away, he watched Todd play ball for his high school in the spring of the next year. They'd still occasionally work out and trash talk each other while playing catch.

He sold the Cobb card because it gave him the creeps. When he held it, he could almost hear the wailing of the demonic fans in the right field stands of Ebbets Field. The sale gave him enough to pay for the remainder of his medical schooling. However, he also did it anonymously and to look at him one would have no idea of his wealth. He continued to keep the other cards in a safe in his apartment, and often forgot he had them. After another rough winter, spring came a bit early. He began more clinical rotations in the hospital, and realized he loved the art of surgery.

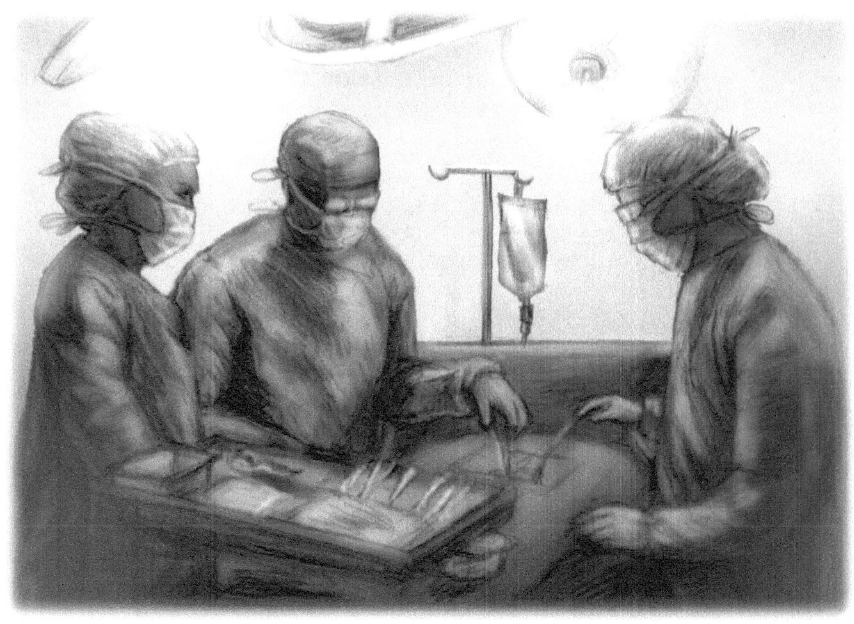

The careful planning and performance of an operation gave him a feeling of satisfaction like nothing else. A couple of weeks into April, Danny was sitting at a nurse's station and glanced at the calendar on the bulletin board. He saw that it was April 15th. It was already late in the day, and he had stayed longer than he should have. He finished his work, signed off the computer, and left the hospital. Although he couldn't say why, he took a cab (not riding the train anymore was the one luxury he allowed himself) over to the National Mall. He was let out at the far end and soon found himself walking up the stairs to the Lincoln Memorial. He reached the top and stood quietly for a moment, looking out across the Mall. He felt a soft, warm breeze come from the inside of the monument. Without turning around, he spoke quietly.

"I knew you'd be here. I don't know how, but I knew."

"I guess that's what happens when friends get to know each other," said Abe, now standing next to him. Danny turned. He saw the young Abe, wearing the same Dodgers hat with a light windbreaker. He looked healthy and strong. People strolled by and didn't bother with a second look as they went to look at the statue of the seated president.

Danny was glad to see Abe looking more vigorous. Before he could comment, Abe spoke first.

"I feel better now that I know my kin are okay. You did me a big favor, helping them out. That boy is a real pistol, and his mother is an angel. I'm so proud of them."

Pointing to the statue behind them, Danny tried to lighten the mood. "If we wouldn't get arrested, I'd get a kick out of taking a picture of you sitting in your own lap."

Lincoln laughed heartily. One or two tourists turned to look briefly and then went on their way. Then he spoke.

"I'm going to miss you, but I'm afraid we won't be seeing each other again for what will be quite some time for you, but only a wink for me. There's a whole town, though, demanding to have you back eventually. I suspect that Jacob won't be able to resist the commotion for long."

It made Danny happy to think about his friends. "I'm looking forward to it."

Abe turned and stared at the statue of himself. "I love America. One of the best things about meeting you was that I felt it was the universe's way of telling me things had turned out all right."

"Well," Danny said apologetically, "You know it's always something in this country."

"Yes, I know", said Abe, "But it will endure. I'm sure of it." He turned away from the statue and looked at Danny, who by now realized that he could feel their time together slipping away one final time.

Abe continued. "You need to know that Christina was heartbroken when she saw you were gone. It was a sad thing to see, and we all felt her grief. I gave Jacob some hell for it, I'll have you know. I could never pin him down as to how, but he said he'd try to fix it."

As he thought of Christina, he felt a sharp tug in his chest. It was an unfamiliar feeling, but somehow strangely reminded him of her. "Maybe that's why I feel so alone," he said, partially to Abe and partially to himself.

Abe nodded, and then started to shimmer with the rays of the late evening sun. Danny could see him start to fade. He heard Abe's voice like a distant echo say, "Well, just don't block my basepath!"

"Then stay away from my base," Danny replied to the empty space next to him. As he turned to walk down the stairs, he was sure he heard the faint sound of laughter.

Epilogue

The summer passed uneventfully, and in the fall, Danny was allowed to finally assist and perform small portions of surgery. His days started at 5 AM, making rounds before heading to the operating room, but he loved every second of it. He'd go home exhausted, but often found he couldn't sleep. He stayed in close touch with Mary and Todd. Every time he saw Todd, he marveled at how much the boy resembled Abe. It made him not miss his friend so much. Still, though, he felt an empty space in his heart.

One evening he stopped at a used bookstore on the way home and saw a familiar-looking volume randomly stacked on a shelf. He picked it up and read the title: *Goblin Market*. He bought it for a dollar and took it home, where he read until he fell asleep. The next day while taking 5 minutes for lunch, he had the unexplained urge to pull up the Georgetown class schedule. He immediately found an evening seminar class entitled "Victorian Poetry". The instructor was not listed, but with a few clicks he signed up.

Two weeks later, he found himself bracing against strong, unusually cold fall winds on the way to the main campus from the hospital. Wishing he'd worn warmer clothes, he consulted the campus map several times and finally found the right building. The seminar started at 7 PM, and the hallway was almost completely dark when he saw an open door at the end, with light streaming into the hall.

He walked into the room and found it empty. He checked his watch to make sure he had the correct date and time. It was 7:05. He figured he was either lost or the class was cancelled.

Tired and cold, he sat down in one of the desks, taking a moment to rest before walking back home. Then he heard the far hallway door slam, and footsteps coming rapidly toward the room. The florescent classroom lights seemed to hum more loudly as the footsteps approached.

With great commotion, a young woman burst through the open door. She wore a heavy full-length jacket, a brightly colored woolen hat, and a thick scarf. The combined effect was almost like a disguise. She carried a large book bag as well as a purse.

She saw him sitting alone, and exclaimed: "Thank God you're here!" She spoke with a strong English accent. She looked as if she were in her mid-twenties, somewhere close to his own age. She put down her bags and turned to him. "Please don't feel awkward, but nobody else signed up for the course. Normally they'd cancel it, but they left it open for some reason. To be honest, I'm here because I need the money. I'm getting my PhD in the English department, and I get a stipend for teaching this class." She paused and caught her breath. "So, please don't drop the course."

Danny didn't know what to say. In all his years of school, he'd never been the only student in a class before and it did make him feel strange. Nonetheless, she seemed sincere to the point of desperation. "I don't intend to drop the course," he replied. "But I may not always be able to make the class. I'm a medical student, and I signed up just to get out of the hospital sometimes."

She was still shivering and kept the hat, coat, and scarf on while she spoke. "That's fine," she said. "Since you're my only student we can make up sessions at your convenience. I really—" she paused again, "*really* need this class."

Danny laughed. "Okay. I'll do my best."

She sat down opposite him. "So why Victorian poetry? That's an odd choice for a medical student."

"I guess so," admitted Danny. "But I had a friend once who introduced me to it and I've never forgotten about it."

She leaned forward, apparently starting to warm up. "Any particular favorite poems?"

He felt a bit shy, but after a pause stated: "Yes."

She leaned back expectantly. "Okay. Title and verse, please."

He cleared his throat. "This is called Echo. It goes like this." He started to recite, "Come to me in the silence of the night…"

She made a slow turn toward him, then cut him off to say the next line. "Come in the speaking silence of a dream…" Her voice trailed off and she stopped. It was quiet for a minute, and the lights hummed in the background.

She stood up and looked at him suspiciously. "Do I know you?" she asked. As she spoke, she pulled off her scarf and reached up, gingerly removing the knit cap. Danny stared as long brown hair tumbled to her shoulders. He immediately recognized her eyes and couldn't stop himself from speaking.

"Christina," he said. "It's me."

When he finished speaking, she looked again at him with mild surprise. "This is getting strange. I go by Tina. Nobody calls me Christina, which is my full name. I must admit, though, that it doesn't sound bad when you say it. You are just so oddly familiar."

"I probably have one of those common faces", said Danny apologetically.

She studied his face and smiled with more warmth. "No, you most certainly don't. It's nice to make your acquaintance." She held her hand out. When he took her hand to shake it, he felt a feeling like warm fire causing ice to melt in his chest. He could see she also felt something unusual as she drew her hand away slowly.

"I was so cold, but now it feels like it's too hot in here," she said. She was flustered and bright red, clearly confused as to what had just happened.

They sat for a long, awkward moment, with neither one wanting the other to leave.

Finally, she spoke again. "Well, since it's just the two of us, I think we can conduct the course however we'd like. How would you feel about trying to warm up with some coffee?"

"Sure," Danny said. "Where?"

She stood and started to put her coat back on, now appearing more comfortable talking with him.

"There's a wonderful coffee and pastry shop a few blocks from campus. I moved here from London two months ago, and would have been completely lost if I hadn't wandered into it the first day I was here. It's the funniest place. It's run by two Frenchmen who are constantly bickering, but it's been open every time I've visited. They don't seem to have any regular hours, and I think they must live there. They make a hot chocolate to die for, and…"

Danny interrupted her. "And I'll bet they have competing racks of insanely delicious pastries."

Just as she finished putting her scarf on, she glanced again at him with a mixture of amusement and alarm. "This is just too crazy. Have you been to this place?"

Danny stood to put his coat on, and suddenly had a feeling that his life was changing for the better.

"I don't know." He answered as truthfully as he could. "Maybe in a dream."

With that, they left the classroom and walked out into the night, discussing their favorite pastries. She reached over and took his arm. After a few steps together, Danny noticed that the stars were shining like a million small spotlights, as if deliberately hung in the sky to show them the way.

PATISSERIE
VICTOR & ALEX